AN ADRENALINE FUELLED
RACE AGAINST THE CLOCK

PERFECT FOR FANS
OF URBAN OUTLAWS

SCAR IS NO ORDINARY
SCHOOLGIRL; AND NO
ORDINARY CAT BURGLAR

IF SCAR MCCALL CAN'T KEEP
HER COOL, THINGS WILL
TURN WILD, AND DANGEROUS,
VERY QUICKLY

AN EXCITING DEBUT FROM
AUTHOR TAMSIN COOKE

HEIST FILE

TARGET:
AZTEC BRACELET

CLIENT:
DESCENDENT OF AN AZTEC PRIEST

ORIGIN:
MEXICO

CENTURY:
SIXTEENTH

MATERIALS:
GOLD AND TURQUOISE

MARKINGS:
ABSTRACT ANIMAL IMAGES CARVED
INTO TURQUOISE STONES

CONDITION:
EXCELLENT

VALUE:
PRICELESS

PREPARE FOR A STORY PACKED WITH PERIL AND PACE...

'The story is exciting, unexpected and a real page turner. It is difficult to guess whether or not Scarlet and her father will ever survive their situation. Even towards the end, you are never quite certain of who can be trusted and who can't. It is still full of sudden unexpected events, especially with the animals.

This book draws you into the story and leaves you wanting to read more. I highly recommend this book and look forward to reading the sequel.'

Roshni, 11

For Violetta and Graham who always believed in me.
For Toby and Daisy who are my inspiration.

OXFORD
UNIVERSITY PRESS

Great Clarendon Street, Oxford, OX2 6DP

Oxford University Press is a department of the University of Oxford.
It furthers the University's objective of excellence in research, scholarship,
and education by publishing worldwide. Oxford is a registered trade mark of
Oxford University Press in the UK and in certain other countries

British Library Cataloguing in Publication Data
Data available

ISBN: 978-0-19-274259-9

1 3 5 7 9 10 8 6 4 2

Printed in Great Britain

Cover and inside illustration: okili77/Shutterstock.com

THE SCARLET FILES

CAT BURGLAR

TAMSIN COOKE

OXFORD
UNIVERSITY PRESS

CHAPTER ONE

I lie flat against the edge of the roof, my senses on high alert. Come on, Dad, where are you? Surely it shouldn't take this long to see if a room is clear. Then a hand clutches my shoulder and my body jumps. Somehow I manage not to fall off the three-storey house. I stare at Dad in amazement. How can he be so quiet? I haven't heard a footstep or even a scuffle on the tiles.

Dad swoops over the lip of the roof, dropping to the second floor balcony below. This is it—the moment I've been waiting for. I take a deep breath and scramble over the guttering. With fingers clinging to the roof, I dangle nine and a half metres above the ground. Adrenalin surging, I swing my legs and hurtle though the air before landing, knees bent, beside him. I rub my arms and stretch out my fingers.

Dad and I are dressed the same—black overalls, balaclavas, thin leather gloves, and rucksacks. Our night-vision goggles make the world green. Together we stare through the glass double doors. The room in front of us is empty, but the owners are sleeping in the next bedroom. Have we woken them? I hate to admit it, but my landing was much louder than Dad's.

Thankfully no lights appear, and Dad picks the lock in the door. Reaching into my back pocket, I pull out a sliver of foil. I hand it to Dad and watch him use it to block the sensor. He slides the door open a fraction, and when the alarm doesn't go off, he yanks it further on its rails.

Dad creeps into the house first and I follow closely behind. He shuts the balcony door, while I take stock of the room. Everything is exactly where I expect it to be— the double bed, the rug, the chest of drawers, the mask, and the jewellery box. Dad's plans were perfect.

I step forward when Dad grabs hold of my arm and jabs his index finger at the large oval rug. My mouth dries. I can't believe I forgot. I give him a quick thumbs-up.

We grab the edge of the rug and carefully roll it back, to reveal small pressure pads dotted about on the carpet. If I'd stepped on one of those, an alarm would have exploded somewhere. Most of the pads are clustered below the spot where the Aztec mask is hanging. Even through my night-vision goggles, the mask looks horrible, frightening. I'm not sure how anyone could sleep with that thing staring down at them.

I watch Dad navigate the room. He pulls some tweezers out of his bag and starts fiddling with various wires. While he deactivates an alarm attached to the mask, I tiptoe across the carpet, avoiding the few pressure pads in my path. My target, the jewellery box, is on top of the chest of drawers. According to Dad's plans, the box is free from alarms, but I finger the area just in case. Good—there are no wires or signs of extra security.

Tilting the wooden lid, I find the box stuffed with brooches, bracelets, and necklaces. I ease some of it to one side when I hear a noise. I freeze. There's another noise—a creak. Someone, somewhere in the house, is moving. I hardly dare breathe. My eyes dart between the door to the landing and Dad, who stands motionless with the Aztec mask in one hand. Dad lifts his free hand, holding it out in front of him. I know what he's telling me: Don't panic. Don't move.

I stay still. Feet scuff the carpet on the landing. Now should we bolt? Again I glance at Dad, but his hand remains in the air. The footsteps pass our door, but that doesn't mean we're safe. What if it's someone collecting a cricket bat to bash us over the heads with? Or phoning the police? I hear a click, and a soft glow of light appears from under the door to the landing. Then I catch the sound of tinkling. I let out a quiet sigh. It's just someone going to the toilet.

Still I don't move and neither does Dad. The tinkling seems to be endless. Finally, I hear a chain flush and a click, and the glow disappears. The footsteps begin again, passing our room, and a bed creaks as someone climbs into it. Dad's hand is still flat against the air. My muscles ache from being so tense. I know he's waiting for the person to fall back to sleep. But really? Do we have to wait this long? At last Dad changes his flat hand into a thumbs-up and twists back around.

As quietly as I can, I dive back into the jewellery box, this time rummaging with more speed. Soon my eyes fall upon a thick bracelet covered in precious stones and I can't contain my grin. I've found it! Fingers shaking, I lift the bracelet, wrap it up in a square of black velvet, and slip it into the front pocket of my rucksack. I pull out an exact replica and stuff it in the bottom of the box. Then I carefully pile on the rest of the jewellery, trying to remember the order in which I took it out. A beaded necklace and dragonfly brooch were definitely on the top. I close the lid, and wipe down every surface I touched. Stepping back, I examine my work. No one will notice . . . hopefully.

I turn around to see Dad reactivating the alarm, now attached to a fake mask hanging on the wall. He wipes down the whole area before hopping over the pressure pads. I meet him by the double bed and together we unroll the rug. Dad studies the room and nods. He uses the foil to stop the sensor, and signals for me to open the door. Slipping outside, I wait for him to join me out on the balcony.

I feel lightheaded. The tension drains away. I can't believe I stole the bracelet . . . all on my own!

Dad relocks the glass doors, as I hoist the rucksack onto my shoulders. Together, under the moonlit sky, we climb over the railings and swing onto the first floor balcony. Without pausing, we leap over another set of railings and drop to the ground. No streetlights—we run to our black car and jump inside.

Dad drives two streets away, before saying, 'NVGs.'

I tear off my night-vision goggles and Dad does the same. He puts on the headlights.

'So what do you think? How did I do?' I burst.

'You were great,' says Dad.

I clasp my gloved hands together. 'When can I do it again?'

'Soon,' says Dad. 'But right now, I think you should try to get some sleep. After all, you do have school tomorrow.'

CHAPTER
TWO

Next morning, the lessons drag and I'm finding it hard to keep my eyes open. At last the bell rings for lunch. I grab my sandwiches, head to the canteen and sit at the far end of a table. As usual empty chairs surround me.

A group of girls fall into the seats at the table behind, laughing and chatting. My heart reels. That would have been me a year ago. I'd have been sitting with Jules and Charlie at my old school, laughing about something stupid. But I haven't seen them for ages. When Dad and I moved, I had to say goodbye . . . and I gave them a fake address. They think I'm living in South Africa. Tears start to prick the corner of my eyes.

Then I give myself a shake. It was my decision to join Dad on his mission. I knew what I was getting into—that I'd have to be cut off from my old life. I push my old friends to the back of my mind, and take another bite of sandwich, when I hear a voice from the table behind.

'You won't believe what I did last night!'

I glance over my shoulder to see a girl grinning madly. I turn back around but her voice drifts over loud and clear.

'Honestly, I had the most amazing night,' she says. 'Andy came over. And we stayed up till like three in the morning and watched two horror films.'

'You didn't?' squeals one of her friends.

'Yeah. Mum and Dad had gone out so . . .'

My lips can't help twitching. Seriously? Watching two horror films with a boy is *amazing*? Thinking about my night, my lips twitch even more. It was the first time Dad allowed me to take an item. Of course I've been on jobs before but I've always been his assistant—holding tools, being lookout, climbing through air vents. But last night he let me locate the bracelet, search for alarms . . .

I fiddle with my hair, reliving every last detail, when all at once I freeze. Something's wrong. The canteen's quiet. I look up and to my horror see that the room is empty. How long have I been here?

The bell rings and I jump to my feet. I can't be late for a lesson. The teachers will notice me. Running down the long hallway I arrive outside my classroom. Thank God I'm not the last one. Joining the stragglers, I drop quietly into my seat in the middle of the room.

Our geography teacher, Mr Anchor, starts droning on about rocks and I try to listen. Leaning on my elbow, I watch him write some geological words on the electronic whiteboard. My eyelids grow heavy, my body warms, my head lowers and before I know it, I'm in the world of dreams.

'Boring you, am I?'

My head jerks up. Mr Anchor is standing directly in front of me, his arms folded. My stomach hits the floor.

'I'm sorry,' I croak. I clear my dry throat. 'I'm sorry,' I say again, sharper this time.

'You've been drooling,' he snaps.

The class bursts out laughing and they strain to look at me. I drop my head and my hair falls over my face. I can't believe this is happening. After a year of making sure I blend into the background, I'm becoming the centre of attention.

'We're reading pages ninety-two to ninety-eight. Do you think you can do that? Or are you likely to fall asleep again?' asks Mr Anchor.

'I can do that,' I mutter, opening my book and flicking through the pages.

'Good!' he says, before returning to the whiteboard.

I avoid looking at anyone; afraid I might catch their eye. I could kick myself . . . or Mr Anchor!

Normally my classmates and teachers don't bother with me. I've made sure that I'm average in lessons, not in the top set or bottom. Even though I've missed a few days staying in safe houses, I've never skipped too much school to be noticeable. I have mousy hair, never wear make-up, and when I'm not in uniform, I dress in plain regular clothes. I haven't made any *real* friends here because I can't let anyone get too close. And to be honest, I find other thirteen-year-old girls pretty boring these days. All they seem to be interested in is music, clothes, make-up, and boys. I like hotwiring cars, defusing alarms, and cracking safes.

For the rest of geography I make sure I pay attention, but I keep an eye on the clock. Come on, 3.15! Eventually the lesson finishes and I grab my bag. Thank God it's the weekend. And after that, I only have two more days of school until it's the summer holidays.

I hurry home to find Dad in the kitchen, with a telephone glued to his ear.

'Sorry,' he mouths, his eyes darting skyward.

By Dad's scowl I know he's talking to his boss, Mr Higgs. Dad works for the magazine *Safe as Houses*. He researches all the latest anti-intruder technology and writes reviews on them. It's his perfect day job.

Leaving Dad to it, I climb the stairs to my room. As ever, it's perfectly tidy; my books stacked in height order; my desk clear of everything apart from the homework I didn't do yesterday; my bench-press loaded with the correct number of weights. Then I notice the corner of a blue scrapbook, peeping out from under my bed. Didn't I put it away properly? If Dad's seen it, he'll kill me. But as I drop to my knees, I relax. Dad never comes into this room.

I'm about to push the scrapbook further under the bed, when my hand hovers. Surely I can take another look. Just one.

Opening the book at the first page, I read the headline: *'Police baffled as Invisible Burglars strike again.'* The newspaper clipping is dated six years ago, when I first found out what Mum and Dad did. Since then I've kept all articles about them . . . and now about Dad and me.

The familiar pang in my chest returns as I think of Mum. She'd brush my hair, and tell me about their heists; how she used glasscutters, how she picked locks. I bite my lip. I reckon I could do some of those things now . . .

Flicking through the pages, I search for the clipping of her last heist, when there's a knock at the door.

My hand freezes.

'Scar, can I come in?' calls Dad.

You're kidding! Dad wants to come into my room? *Now?* I shove the scrapbook under my bed and grab my English homework before leaping onto the top of the duvet, as if I was sitting here all along.

'Scar, can I come in?' he calls again, louder this time.

'Sure.'

Dad walks in with a large bag dangling from one hand and a medicine box full of insulin for his diabetes in the other. He must have just injected. I glance up at his face. He looks serious. Oh no! He's seen the scrapbook!

'Is everything OK?' I ask, waiting for the explosion.

He rubs his forehead, then says, 'How was school?'

Of all the things I expected him to say, this was the last. We don't tend to talk about anything other than, well . . . cat burglary. 'I fell asleep in Geography,' I say, with a shrug.

'Oh?' says Dad, dropping into the chair at my desk. 'I guess that's my fault. Another late night.'

'I don't mind.'

'I know *you* don't. But your mother would.'

I glance at the only photograph in my room on top of my bedside table: the one of Mum with her arms around me. We're wearing matching T-shirts and caps with the logo for Born Wild on them. She used to work for the animal charity and I helped her whenever I could.

'She would have been proud of you,' says Dad. 'You did well last night.'

'I did?'

'You know you did!'

My face splits into a grin.

'You were a real professional,' he continues. 'You didn't panic when that person got up, you waited, and you—'

'Actually Dad, I've been thinking. I was wondering if I could start doing a bit more.'

His eyebrows rise.

'I could do a job on my own, just a little one. You could stay in the car. I'd pick the locks, get the items, and—'

'Scar, it's one thing to collect an item on your own. It's a whole different dimension, breaking into a house on your own.'

'But—'

'We've been through this before. You're too young, you're not ready and you've got much more to learn.'

I open my mouth to speak but Dad lifts his hand to silence me. 'Anyway, I need a favour. That was Higgs on the phone and he's on his way here with some burglar alarm for me to look at. I need you to put these things into the safe.'

He opens his bag, and pulls out the mask and bracelet from last night. I want to argue with him. I want to let him know that I'm more than ready to do a job on my own, but I can see from his expression it would be pointless.

'Fine,' I say with a sigh, taking the bracelet and mask from him. I'm surprised how heavy they are. I hadn't noticed yesterday. 'Are these really Aztec artefacts?'

Dad nods. 'From the 1500s.'

'Wow!'

'Wow indeed! They were stolen from a Mexican temple a few years ago. It's time they went back.'

I stand up, ready to move into the lounge, when Dad's watch beeps and a red light flashes on and off. The outside sensors have been activated. Someone is on our driveway.

'I don't believe it. That must be Higgs. He must have been on his mobile in the car,' says Dad, pressing a button on his watch, stopping the alarm. He grimaces at the mask and bracelet. 'You don't have time to get these into the safe. You're going to have to look after them here in your bedroom.'

'Will that be all right? I mean . . . will this be secure enough?'

Dad glances around. 'You know what? This room is probably the best place in the house. Higgs won't come in here.'

The doorbell rings and he throws me a thin smile before leaving the room. I hear him open the front door and start speaking. His words are muffled. I don't bother straining to hear what is being said. Instead, I wander in front of the floor-length mirror and hold the Aztec mask to my face. Why would anyone want this? It's horrible!

The mask is made out of wood, shaped like an over-sized human skull. The eyes are big black circles, surrounded with white shell. Holes have been cut out of the middle of each of them, and with my eyes peeking through the whole thing looks sinister.

The rest of the mask is covered in a mosaic of turquoise stones. Some are missing. Most are cracked. In the centre of the forehead is a deep hole where a larger stone must have once lived. A jewel perhaps? There's a leering mouth with . . .

My heart jumps. Are those *real* teeth? Was this mask made from *real* animal teeth?

I quickly put the mask on my desk and look at the bracelet instead. It's far more beautiful, but then, that isn't hard! It's a bangle, an inch thick and slightly mis-shapen, as if someone has tried to crush it in their fist. It's made out of finely woven gold, like spun silk, and has five bright turquoise stones running around the outside. Each stone, the size of a twenty-pence piece, has been shaped into a creature. One resembles a bird with large wings, but I can't make out the others. They're too abstract, with bumps that could be legs or tails. It's weird that this bracelet is five hundred years old. The turquoise and gold look far too shiny and new, especially compared to the stones on the mask.

Without thinking, I slip my hand through it. I lift my arm into the air and the gold and turquoise seem to shine even brighter. I can't believe I found this in a box full of ordinary jewellery. It's too precious and valuable. In fact, it's so precious and valuable I should take it off.

I grab hold of the bracelet and pull, expecting it to slip off as easily as it slipped on. Yet the bracelet doesn't move. I yank again, harder this time but still it refuses to budge. Each time I pull, my skin is dragged with it. I stare closely at the bracelet. The gold is now flush against my skin. How is that possible? It was bigger than my hand seconds ago.

Then all of a sudden, I feel pain, as if sea urchin spines are stabbing my skin. I want to scream, but I can't. Dad's boss is in the lounge. I clamp my lips shut and try to pry my fingers under the gold. I want to pull the brace-let away, but my nails can't get an edge . . . there is no edge. The gold is sinking into my skin. The throbbing intensifies and I scratch frantically at my wrist. The gold is getting paler, the turquoise more translucent.

Then my stomach crumbles. For the bracelet van-ishes completely. The pain stops, but I feel dizzy, weak. I fall backwards onto the bed, my body growing clammy. I lie there motionless. How long I lie, I'm not sure. At some point I hear a knock on the door but I can't even open my mouth to speak.

'Thank goodness Higgs has left,' says Dad stepping into the room. Instantly he's beside my bed. 'Scar, what is it? Are you ill?'

I feel the back of his hand against my head, but my eyes refuse to focus.

'Scar, what's wrong?' he demands.

At last I manage to open my mouth. In a small croaky voice, I say, 'The bracelet. It's gone.'

CHAPTER THREE

I sit at the kitchen table, staring at my wrist. Scratches cover my skin, blood oozes out, but there's no sign of any gold or turquoise. My stomach churns. How could a bracelet disappear inside me?

'Well, I give up, I can't find it anywhere,' says Dad, walking into the kitchen. He's spent the last half hour searching my bedroom.

'I told you—you wouldn't. Because I didn't drop it. I didn't hide it. All I did was put it on.'

'I know that's what you sai— what have you been doing to your arm?' Dad is suddenly by my side.

'I was trying to find the bracelet,' I say. 'But don't worry, I've stopped now. I've given up.'

'You were trying to rip your skin to find it?' Dad falls into the seat next to me, and his eyes bore into mine.

'You're telling the truth, aren't you?'

'Yes! When have I ever lied to you before?'

'You haven't.' He stretches out his arm towards me and then hesitates. 'May I?'

I nod.

Prodding my skin gently, he says, 'I can't feel anything hard in there.'

'That's because it's disappeared.'

Dad glances up at the ceiling and shakes his head. 'I must be going mad because for some strange reason, I believe you.'

'You do?'

'Yes, I believe you put it on.' He stares at my arm and frowns. 'But I don't think it disappeared inside you. I think the bracelet was too old and not looked after properly. The gold must have disintegrated once it touched your skin.'

'Is that even possible? What about the turquoise?'

'Of course it's possible! The stones must have disintegrated too.'

I get the impression Dad is trying to convince himself just as much as he's trying to convince me.

He rubs his forehead. 'Anyway, we've got a bigger problem to deal with now.'

'We do?' What on earth could be bigger that a bracelet vanishing into my skin?

'We've got to tell our clients they can only have the mask,' says Dad.

OK—we do have a big problem.

'Come on, I need your help,' he says, scraping back his chair. 'I need to get their details again.'

I follow Dad into our lounge, over to the large log burner in the fireplace. There's a gold-framed mirror hanging above, and as Dad approaches it, I see his reflection. His face is grim.

'Can't you just call up the client and say we didn't find the bracelet yesterday?' I say. 'Can't you say it wasn't where we thought it would be?'

Dad shakes his head. 'I couldn't even if I wanted to. I contacted them late last night. They already know the raid was a success.'

Dad positions his fingers around the base of the log burner while I grip the other end. Usually log burners are fitted, heavy, and impossible to move without serious strength. But ours has been custom-built and together we pull it to one side. I step into the place where the log burner was and stand up, my top half now hidden inside the chimney breast. The hole is quite big for me but it's a tight squeeze for Dad.

He presses a torch into my hand and I perch on tiptoes. I pour light onto the metal box built into the wall and enter the code into the electronic keypad. The door to the safe springs open. Grabbing Dad's laptop bag, I close the door and relock it. Then I bend down and climb out.

'Oh . . . do you want me to put the mask in there too?' I ask, remembering.

'No, I think I'll keep the mask where I can see it.'

My gut wrenches and I feel my cheeks flush. 'I'm sorry, Dad. I really am.'

'I know you are,' he says. 'Why don't you go and get some fresh air? I can do this on my own.'

'Or . . . I could help?'

Dad takes the laptop from me. 'I don't think so. The less you know about this, the safer you are. And if I were you, after all that has happened, I wouldn't pester me now.'

I nod but my eyes remain fixed on the computer. How I would love to learn Dad's secrets about his clients and the jobs he's carried out. But he won't even tell me his password.

'Go on, get out,' he says, nodding towards the doorway.

'Fine! I'm going.'

I slip out of the front door. We moved here just under a year ago. It's a three-bedroomed detached house with a garage—the perfect size for someone on Dad's daytime salary. If we lived in a mansion, Mr Higgs would ask questions. There are six grey stone houses in our cul-de-sac, built twenty years ago. Ours has the best location, since it backs onto woodland—great for sneaking in and out. All six front gardens look the same, with flowering shrubs running around the outside of neat lawns, and the odd tree dotted here and there. Everyone else in our street is over the age of seventy-five. They keep to themselves, which suits us just fine.

The street is empty. I wander halfway down, not knowing where I'm heading, just that I have to give Dad some

19

space. Besides, he was right—I need fresh air. I would love to believe Dad's explanation of the bracelet disintegrating, but deep down I know what I saw. Glaring at my wrist, I drift along. That's when I hear it. I stop and hear it again. A scared, pitiful meow. I find myself peering into number four's garden. Mrs Riley's. Creeping over some shrubs, I stand on the grass. Another screechy meow comes from somewhere above. I look up and spot grey fur hidden amongst the top branches of a large oak tree.

'You're stuck!'

The cat meows, sounding more helpless than ever.

I glance at Mrs Riley's lounge window, and see tight grey curls peeping over the top of an armchair. She's watching the TV on the opposite wall. Her screen is so enormous, I can watch the programme from over here, and I can hear it too. The volume must be on its highest setting.

The cat meows again. I know I shouldn't use my skills during daylight, but there's no way I can leave it stuck up there. Looking around, I see our close is still empty. I dart towards the tree. There aren't many branches low down, but there are nodules sticking out of the trunk. My fingers and feet find them easily as I scramble up to the first set of branches. Then I swing from one bough to another until I'm at the top. A silvery-grey cat clings to a high branch, trembling and mewing.

'It's all right. S'all right,' I say, in a soothing voice, stretching out my arm, rubbing my fingertips together, beckoning the cat towards me.

The cat hisses.

'Don't be scared. Come here.'

Its tail waves to and fro.

'Am I honestly going to have to come and get you?' I crawl along the branch but the stupid cat treads backwards away from me. 'Don't do that, you'll fall.'

The cat steps backwards again. The branch sways, threatening to break. I have no choice. I swing forward and swipe the cat off the branch. It wrestles in my grip, scratching and spitting. But somehow I manage to cling onto it, leaping from bough to bough. As soon as I'm back on the lawn, I throw the cat to the ground. It hurtles away, its fur sticking up on end as if it's been electrocuted.

'Ungrateful cat!' I snap, rubbing my arms.

When suddenly the hairs on the back of my neck shoot up. I sense someone watching me. I look through Mrs Riley's lounge window, but she's still facing the TV. I look through the other windows, higher up, and catch a rush of blond hair before it disappears. My heart thrashes. Someone is in that room. And that someone must have seen me scale a tree.

I race back home, bursting into the lounge. 'Dad, does someone live with Mrs Riley? I thought she lived alone.'

'She does live alone,' says Dad. 'Why?'

I pause. I've already caused Dad enough trouble today. He'd think even worse of me if he knew I scaled a tree in front of someone. 'Oh it's nothing. How . . . how did you get on with the client?'

Dad shakes his head. 'They're not impressed. They kept going on and on about how they're going to have to let down *their* client in Mexico now. *Their* client, a descendent of an Aztec priest, who's been searching for these artefacts all his life.'

My chest tightens in guilt. 'That bracelet belongs in Mexico,' I mumble, but I don't think Dad hears.

He rubs his forehead. 'So anyway, they're demanding a discount.'

'Well . . . that's fair enough isn't it? They're only getting half the goods.'

'Yes,' says Dad slowly. 'But that's not all they want. They want us to do another job too.'

'Really?' I say in surprise. 'That means they still trust us.'

'Or they're taking advantage of the situation.'

'But we can easily do another job for them—why do you look so worried?'

'Because,' says Dad, clearing his throat, 'they want us to do it in eleven days.'

I stare at him, without blinking. 'Eleven days? Why so soon? And why so specific?'

Dad shrugs.

'But that's not enough time.'

'I tried telling them that, but they were very insistent. I'm sorry, Scar, under these circumstances I had to accept. Our target is Mr Harlington, a city banker. And a week next Tuesday, we *have* to steal a sculpture of a double-headed serpent from him.'

Dad looks uneasy. I feel uneasy. Something is very wrong about this.

CHAPTER FOUR

The next eleven days fly by. I hardly sleep, but luckily school breaks up for the holidays. In the dead of night I scale trees in the woods behind our house. And in the day, Dad tests me endlessly on the layout of the Harlingtons' house, including the positions of the surveillance cameras. He obtained the house plans earlier in the week from the planning office, and the next day he entered their property. Using his *Safe as Houses* ID, he pretended to check out their security system, while really hiding cameras in every room. Dad hardly ever does this, since it's so risky, but this time he didn't have a choice.

Now he's come up with a way we can get into the house. Well, when I say we—I mean me! I've got to get in and then let him in. The words 'be careful what you wish for' seem to be haunting me. I know I wanted to do a job

23

on my own, but this one is so huge and rushed. And after what happened with the bracelet, we can't afford to make a mistake. Plus I can't get rid of that uneasy feeling.

Too soon, the morning of the job arrives. I wake up ridiculously early with a churning stomach. I try to go back to sleep but my brain's too busy, working out the ways this burglary can go wrong. In the end, I dress in jeans and a T-shirt and creep down the stairs. I don't want to wake Dad. He likes to lie in on heist days.

I help myself to a bowl of cereal when I hear a beeping coming from the counter top. I push Dad's medicine box to one side, and find his watch lying upside down, flashing red. He's obviously forgotten to take it to his bedroom, but right now, that's not my concern. Someone is on our driveway or in our front garden. I switch off the alarm and notice the time. It's only six o'clock.

I sneak into the lounge on all fours and peer over the windowsill. The same grey cat I fetched from the tree prowls across our front lawn. But that can't have set off the alarm. The sensors are too high, at least waist height. Then I spy a tall boy coming out from under the trailing branches of our willow tree. He has blond spiky hair . . . the same blond hair I spotted in Mrs Riley's top window.

I watch the boy walk over to the cat and pick it up. I wait for him to leave, but to my horror, he turns, looks me straight in the eyes and waves. Then he wanders up the garden path, heading straight for our front door. Before he can ring the bell and wake Dad, I race to open it. Sliding outside, I close the door behind me.

'Hi,' says the boy, grinning. 'I know it's early, but I was fetching my cat.'

He appears to be the same age as me, although he's much taller. He has bright green eyes and the palest skin I've ever seen.

I smile blandly, not wanting to make an impression.

'You're Sarah, aren't you? That's what my gran says.'

'Who's your gran?' I ask, not bothering to correct him.

'Janice Riley,' he replies, pointing to house number four. 'I'm staying with her for the summer. My parents have gone on a cruise.'

Oh no! He really is the boy from the top window . . . but maybe he won't recognize me. Maybe he didn't even see me climb the tree. I force another bland smile.

The cat wriggles in his grasp and hisses at me.

'Sorry,' says the boy, tightening his grip. 'Sphinx doesn't like anyone. I'm not sure she even likes me,' he adds, as the cat's claws dig into his arm.

Sphinx wriggles again and this time she squirms free. She lands on the ground and stalks off, her tail frozen in the air.

'I've been wanting to thank you for rescuing her the other day, but I haven't seen you around.'

'What?' I say, my voice shriller than usual.

'I saw you climb that tree. It was amazing. I've never seen anyone climb like that before. I was wondering what I was going to do to get her. I was even thinking about ringing the fire brigade, and then you—'

'It was nothing,' I say, twisting my head around, looking at the closed door. Don't let Dad hear this!

'It was not nothing. You were like a monkey. No, you were like Spider-Man.'

'It was nothing,' I repeat. 'I just heard your cat screech and climbed up and got her.'

The boy gives me a funny look. 'You couldn't have heard her screech. Sphinx is a mute.'

'No, she's not. She's a screechy thing. I heard her meowing half way down the street.'

'I'm telling you, she's a mute. That's why I chose her. I felt sorry for her.'

'Maybe she just doesn't like talking to you!' I say.

The boy laughs, but I don't join in. Finally he says, 'You must have heard her scrabbling about. You probably heard her claws on the branches.'

Yeah! Because that really sounds like a meow! I'm about to open my mouth and argue when I come to my senses. I just need him to leave. 'Thanks for saying thank you. I guess I'll see you aro—'

'So what else is there to do around here apart from climb trees?' says the boy. 'I haven't got much to do this summer and Gran doesn't want me hanging around the house all the time.'

Well, you're not hanging around me! 'People from my school go to a park on the other side of the village. You should go see what they're up to. They often play football.'

'I don't like football,' says the boy. I must have looked surprised because he adds, 'I like rugby.'

'They play rugby too.'

'Actually Dad wants me to like rugby. I like computers.' His eyes start to gleam. 'I like computer games of course, but I prefer programming. Mum's a computer programmer. She often works in California.'

Ah! He's a computer geek. That explains the pale skin.

'But there's this one game I've got,' he continues. 'Mum's just sent it to me. You get to fight zombies. You can come round and play it if you like?'

Really? This boy is not getting the hint to leave me alone!

'Are you doing anything later?' he asks.

Luckily I don't have to answer, because a black van drives into our close. It pulls up at the edge of my front garden. Large yellow letters, *Parcel Deliveries*, are plastered across the outside. That's weird. It's a bit early for a delivery, isn't it? Then it occurs to me what it must be bringing—the replica double-headed snake. Delivery companies bring forgeries for about half of Dad's jobs.

The driver's door opens and a guy, about eighteen years old, with a black quiff and designer stubble jumps out. I glare at his leather jacket. *Cow murderer!*

He strolls round the back of the van, and reappears with a cardboard box, the size of a microwave oven. He wanders towards us and my hand immediately flies to my nose. What is that smell? It's like a dead rat I once found. What is in that box? Please say it's not a real decomposing snake!

I glance at the boy to see his reaction, but his nose isn't even wrinkling. Can't he smell it or is he just being amazingly polite?

My eyes water. I wait for the guy to apologize about the smell. He doesn't. His eyes gloss over me and fall onto the boy.

'I'm looking for Mr McCall,' he says, his words lazy, drawn out.

The boy beside me shrugs and I step forward. Taking my hand away from my nose and trying not to breathe, I say, 'I'm Mr McCall's daughter. Can I take it?' *Not that I want to!*

'If you're his daughter, then I don't see why not.'

Again I expect him to mention the smell, but he simply puts the box down and pulls out an electronic keypad from his pocket. 'Print and sign here.'

I scribble my name twice using the stylus and hand him back the keypad. Bending my knees, I grab hold of the parcel. I wish I could hold my nose too.

'Would you like some help?' says the guy. 'It's rather heavy for a girl.'

'Maybe I'm strong for a girl,' I snap, plucking the parcel into the air. I can see why some people would think it was heavy, but hours of doing pull-ups mean it's fine for me. Then I notice the guy's eyes narrow. I let my arms buckle. 'Yeah, it is quite heavy,' I whimper.

'Do you want me to take it in for you?' asks the boy.

'No, I think I can manage. But I'd better go in now.'

'Make sure your Dad gets it,' says the guy. He checks

the screen on his keypad before adding, 'Scarlet.' He then walks away.

'I thought you said your name was Sarah,' says the boy.

'It's Scarlet,' I say, pretending to stagger as I turn around.

Then I realize the smell is disappearing . . . which means it didn't come from the box . . . which means it must have come from the delivery guy. Glancing over my shoulder, I see him disappear into the van. Does he not care about his stench? With his perfect hair and stubble, he looks like the kind of guy who would.

'Are you sure I can't help you carry it?' says the boy. 'It's not a problem.'

I shake my head. 'You could open the door for me.'

'My name's Ethan, by the way,' he says, pulling the handle.

'Well, thanks, Ethan. Could you close it now?'

The door shuts, and I'm about to hoist the parcel higher into my arms, when a voice says, 'Where are you taking it?'

I whisk my head around to see Ethan standing inside our hallway, the door closed behind him. I glance up the stairs, looking out for Dad. 'What . . . what are you *doing* in here?'

'I thought you wanted me to come in. Oh! You wanted me to close the door after you,' says Ethan, his cheeks reddening. 'I guess I'll see you around then,' he adds, before darting out of the house.

Luckily there's still no sign of Dad as I hurry into the kitchen. I put the box onto the table and tear it open. The Aztec double-headed serpent is in great condition, much better than the mask was. More like the bracelet. As soon as I think of the golden band, the familiar sickening tug returns to my stomach. I force the bracelet to the back of my mind and concentrate on the sculpture instead. It's carved out of wood, and covered with turquoise mosaic. The two heads on either end have red shells for their noses and mouths, and *thankfully* no real animal teeth; just conch shells for fangs.

'It's arrived then. I was beginning to think we'd have to postpone,' says Dad, stepping into the kitchen. His eyes are bleary and his brown hair sticks up in all directions. 'How are you feeling anyway?'

'I'm OK.'

Dad grabs a mug and holds it beneath the coffee machine. 'The first time you break into a house on your own can be scary, but I know you'll do fine.'

I try to smile at him. At the same time I try to forget his words from last week when he told me I wasn't ready. I know the only reason I'm doing the break-in tonight is because there is no other choice.

'You *will* do fine,' he repeats.

Who's he's trying to convince—him or me?

CHAPTER FIVE

I only hope Dad is right, as I stand eighteen hours later in a narrow alleyway behind a row of houses. We are in Belgravia, one of the richest areas in London. The Harlingtons' house is a grand middle terrace, four floors high and coated in white stucco.

Dad and I are dressed the same as last time—all in black, NVGs, and rucksacks—except this time, we carry more tools. I crane my neck all the way back to glimpse the top of the house and groan inwardly. Why can't rich people live in bungalows?

'I've disabled their exterior alarm and CCTV,' whispers Dad. 'You know what to do?'

I nod.

'Then I'll see you at the front door.'

Dad slopes away, leaving me beside the perimeter

31

wall. Come on, I can do this. Dad's counting on me. Plus if it all goes well, who knows what he'll let me do next.

I scramble over the tall stone wall and drop into the Harlingtons' back garden. Running into the centre of the lawn, I open my rucksack and pull out a gas-pressured grappling hook. My hands tremble. I have only one real chance at this. If I miss, the hook will make too much noise scraping over the roof.

Looking through the sight hole, I aim at the chimney, and pull the trigger. There's a soft pop. The grappling hook shoots into the air from the barrel, trailing a steel wire behind. The hook grabs onto the chimney and my insides squeal. It worked. I tug twice to make sure it doesn't come loose, before running to the back of the house. The chimney's no longer in view but I can see the wire dangling beside the wall.

Holding the grappling device in both hands, I take a deep breath and plant my feet against the stucco. Then leaning backwards, until I'm almost horizontal, I walk up the back of the house. Step after step, higher and higher, the wire retracting with every pace. If only Ethan could see me now. I really am Spider-Man!

As soon as my feet touch the edge of the roof, I pull harder, making my body almost vertical. I advance up the sloping roof to the chimney, then release the grappling hook and stuff it into my rucksack. Whoa! I've just climbed over eleven metres. But I don't have time to relax.

The skylight is about a car-length away on the other side of the roof. I creep towards it, my fingers clinging to the tiles, my toes finding every possible ledge to perch on. The glass pane is connected to its frame by hinges halfway down the sides. As Dad predicted, it's slightly ajar. Sliding my fingers under the rim at the base, I pull the window towards me. It pivots like a see-saw, leaving greater gaps at the top and bottom.

The window leads to a small bathroom used by one of Mr Harlington's sons. I squeeze through the gap at the base. Even though it's open as far as possible, there's no way Dad would have fitted. Once through, I hold onto the edge of the window frame and dangle two metres in the air. Unclasping my fingers I fall to the marble below. My trainers hit stone. Noooo! I missed the rug. I wait, blood pumping in my ears. Let the Harlingtons be deep sleepers.

No sounds emerge and I inch over to the open doorway. The landing's empty. I tiptoe past another of the boys' rooms and down a flight of stairs. I stand outside Mr Harlington's bedroom, staring at the alarm flush against the wall. It's activated—the green light's flashing on the panel. The second alarm, positioned by the front door, must be the same.

The last time Dad was in the house, he stuck an infrared wireless surveillance camera, the size of a five-pence piece, onto an ornate picture frame on the opposite wall. Dad worked out the code by scrutinizing Mr Harlington's fingers every time he dialled the alarm.

I enter the code and the green light turns red. Pocketing the surveillance camera, I sweep down the remaining stairs and stand on the bottom step in the entrance hall. The alarm system beside the front door is blinking red too.

I know I'm safe . . . I should be safe . . . oh, let me be safe. Holding my breath, I step onto the ground floor. I wait for the explosion of sound but nothing happens. Letting out a huge sigh, I hurry over to the front door, and carefully pull back the first bolt. It screeches against its fittings. I pull the second and third bolts back—both seem to be just as deafening. I look up the stairs but thankfully no one seems to have heard. I turn the latch and open the door, allowing Dad to slip through, before closing it again. Neither of us speaks.

Dad slides the welcome mat backwards, and pulls open a trapdoor to reveal a safe with a rotary combination lock; the sort of lock that needs twisting to the left and right. The safe has been placed in the hole with its door facing upwards. Dad retrieves his stethoscope from his rucksack and I gaze at it. Couldn't I have one go? One shot? If it didn't work, I'd stop and Dad could carry on.

Dad puts the headset in his ears and holds the chestpiece to the safe. He manipulates the combination lock, listening for clicks, when he stops and looks up at me. Even though a balaclava covers his face, I know he's frowning. He lifts both hands into the air and jabs his index fingers at various rooms. I know what he's telling me: *get on with it*.

Reluctantly I turn around. I grab a surveillance camera off the yucca plant in the hallway and drop it into my rucksack. I then close my eyes, visualizing the whereabouts of the other nineteen. Dad put them on the ground floor only; apart from the one I got upstairs. He assumed, correctly as usual, that the safe would be on the ground floor as this was the only level alarmed.

Methodically and almost soundlessly, I dart from room to room. I run from kitchen to dining room, cloak-room to drawing room. I find cameras on bookshelves, curtain poles, and sculptures. Soon I have only one room to go—the study. It's at the far end of the house, the furthest point from the sleeping Harlingtons.

I tiptoe down the long corridor and reach for the door handle . . . when my stomach heaves. I slam my hand over my mouth and nose. The smell is familiar. I stare at the closed door, recoiling in horror. It's the smell of death, of decomposing rats like the delivery guy. My eyes water and saliva wells up in the back of my throat. I want to turn around, run back to Dad. But I can't. I have to be professional. I have to get to that surveillance camera.

Forcing my fingers to turn the handle, I push open the door and stumble into the room. I cannot believe what I'm seeing, and before I can stop myself, a huge growl rips from the back of my throat. It reverberates around the room, around the house. Then my legs crumple and I sink to the floor.

CHAPTER
SIX

I try to stand, but my limbs are shaking. I can't take my eyes off the scene in front of me—the scene of death. A rhino horn hangs on the wall and a tiger skin lies on the floor. These animals have died for the Harlingtons' art. My heart pounds. I no longer feel sick. I feel something far worse. I lift up my chin, open my mouth and roar, louder and longer this time.

Feet pound the corridor, but I don't care. Let it be the Harlingtons. I sweep my gloved hands across the oak floor, my nails scratching deep grooves into the wood.

I glare at the rhino horn. I want to—no, I *need* to— rip it off the wall. How dare it be on display? I clamber to my feet just as someone bursts into the room. I snarl. It isn't Mr Harlington.

Dad runs to my side 'Are you OK?' he whispers. 'I heard an animal.'

'Have you seen what's in here?' I demand.

'Quiet! You'll wake the Harlingtons,' hisses Dad, glancing at the open door we came through.

Good. Let them come. Then I can . . .

Dad grabs hold of my arm and I wrench it free.

'Scar, what is wrong with you?'

I jab my finger in the direction of the horn and then the rug, my mouth filling with venom.

'You want them? They're not what we're here for.'

'No, I don't want them!' I exclaim.

'Shhh,' says Dad, slamming one finger to his mouth.

'They sicken me!'

'They sicken me too,' says Dad. 'But right now, we have to get out of here. Did you get the camera?'

'I don't care about the camera.'

Dad throws his hands in the air. 'Well, I do.' He glances back at the open door before running sound-lessly to the uplighter in the corner. He plucks the camera off the rim and says, 'I've got it.'

'Good for you!'

Dad grabs hold of my arm and bundles me out of the room. 'Was the door closed when you came in?' he whispers.

I shrug.

'Scar, I'm asking you a question. Was the door closed?'

'Yes!' I snap. I take one last look at the rug on the floor, and lift back my head ready to roar again, when Dad closes the door.

My anger instantly evaporates. The smell of death lingers but all of a sudden, I remember why we're here, what we have to do. 'Oh God,' I whisper, clasping my hands to my mouth. 'Have I woken them?'

'I hope not.' Dad plants his hands on my shoulders, and through his NVGs looks me straight in the eyes. 'Are you up for this? Or do I need to find us another way out?'

'I'm up for it.'

'Then from now on, no more talking!'

Dad and I run back down the corridor, through the music room, the lounge, the dining room. We stop at the bottom of the staircase, beside the welcome mat that is now back in its proper place. We look up the stairs, listening for sounds, watching out for movement. When nothing emerges, I let out a quiet sigh. Thank God the Harlingtons are deep sleepers. Thank God that weird noise—whatever it was, wherever it came from—happened at the far end of the house.

Dad eases the front door open and exits. I close the door behind him and pull the three bolts back into place as quietly as I can. I tiptoe up one flight of stairs until I'm outside the Harlingtons' bedroom again. Their snuffles drift towards me, and an image of a horn and skin flies into my brain. My fists clench. I want to enter their room and . . . I shake my head. What am I thinking? I just have to get out of here.

I uncurl my fist, ready to tap in the numbers to reactivate the alarm, when fear ripples through me. I look at my fingers in horror. My nails have ripped through the tips of my gloves. They're long, pointed, claw-like. Then right before my eyes, they shrink and disappear back into my gloves.

What the . . . ? Then I hear a snore from the other side of the door. I don't have time to think about this. I punch the numbers on the panel and the alarm switches from red to green.

I sneak up the remaining staircase, along the corridor and back into the bathroom. The window is still wide open. I climb onto the edge of the bath and bend my legs. Taking a deep breath, I spring into the air, my fingers grasping the rim of the windowsill. Using all of my strength, I pull myself through, until once more I'm standing on the roof.

I push the windowpane, pivoting it back into place, leaving only a narrow gap. My back drips with sweat and beads trickle down my face. I want nothing more than to rip off my NVGs and balaclava, feel the cool air on my skin. But I can't. Not yet.

Scrambling over to the chimney, I pull out a second, more complex grappling hook from my rucksack. I set the electronic timer on the hook to two minutes, before fastening it to a brick at the top of the chimney. I have exactly one hundred and twenty seconds before the hook unclasps and flies back into the handle device. I race over to the edge of the roof and toss the device over the side. Dad set the wire at eleven metres, so the handle at the end of the cable won't hit the floor and make a noise.

Holding onto the wire, I throw myself over the ledge of the roof and abseil down the house. Reaching the handle, I jump the remaining metre to the ground. Seconds later, the grappling hook shoots towards the handle. I drop it quickly so the wire doesn't slice off my finger.

I pick it back up, shove it into my rucksack and hurtle through the garden. I climb over the wall and run down the alleyway, meeting Dad at the far end of the street. He points to the car and I race towards it, leaving him to reactivate the Harlingtons' CCTV and exterior alarms.

I fling myself into the car and wait. Leaning my head against the seat, my mind whirrs. What happened to me back there? Where did that roar come from? I clutch my stomach. And what happened to my nails? Did I imagine that? I look at my gloves and my stomach plummets. There are definite rips at the ends where the fingertips should be. But nails don't just grow. I must have scraped off the tips when I abseiled down the house. Yeah—that must be it.

The driver's door opens and Dad leaps inside. He starts the ignition and in complete darkness we pull away. After half a minute we peel off our balaclavas and NVGs, and Dad switches on the headlights. I breathe deeply, relishing the cool air on my face. Then I realize Dad hasn't spoken.

'I'm sorry,' I say.

Still there's silence.

'I . . . I don't know what happened. I just got so angry.'

'I don't know what happened either,' says Dad, his voice tight.

My insides churn. 'It won't happen again.'

'I know it won't.' His fingers squeeze the steering wheel. 'I'm not sure I can take you on another job again.'

'What? That's not fair. We completed it, didn't we? You got the sculpture and we didn't get caught.'

'We only just made it. You could have woken them up. And if I hadn't found you, you probably would have.' Dad pauses before adding, 'You were unprofessional. Your mother hated fur too, but there is no way she would have jeopardized a job like that.'

I feel a wave of nausea, when I spot a light flashing through Dad's black sleeve. 'Your watch,' I exclaim.

'What?'

'Your watch—it's flashing red.'

Dad takes a hand off the steering wheel and pulls back his sleeve. The red light on his watch shines out in the darkness. He turned off the volume earlier.

'Someone's on our driveway or in the garden,' I say.

'Oh that's just great!' snaps Dad, slamming his foot on the accelerator. 'This is turning out to be one heck of a night!'

The journey home is in silence. Bright lights of cities and towns melt away as we speed down motorways and main roads. We turn off into our village and Dad pulls to the side of the road, cutting the headlights.

'Put on your head gear,' he says.

'Do I have to? It's probably just an animal.'

'Scar, how many times do I have to tell you? Don't take unnecessary risks.'

I gulp. I know he isn't just talking about now. I pull the balaclava and NVGs back on, and Dad does the same. He drives the car slowly into our cul-de-sac, keeping the throb of the engine low, and parks outside number three.

'I need to know I can trust you. I need to know you'll do as I say,' he says. 'And right now—I need you to stay here. If I don't come back in half an hour, you know what to do.'

'Can't I come?'

'No!' he says, slipping out of the car.

As soon as he's out of eyeshot, I open my door and creep down the street. Our house is in complete darkness. There are no lights coming from any room and it looks exactly how we left it. Dad's being over-cautious, I'm sure. But where is he? Then I spot him peering through one of the downstairs windows.

I jump over the hedges running around the edge of our garden, and hide beneath the trailing branches of the willow tree, not taking my eyes off Dad.

Then all of a sudden he spins around, and runs in my direction. His feet pound the ground. He isn't even trying to be quiet.

'What's wrong?' I whisper, poking my head out of the branches.

Dad leaps into the air. At the same time, he pulls back his arm, releasing it forward as if to punch me. I jump backwards and Dad's hand stop centimetres from my face.

'What are you doing here?' he yelps. 'I told you to stay in the car.'

Before I can answer, he grabs my arm and yanks me back through the hedges with him.

'To the car,' he says, dragging me down the street.

'Dad, what—'

A gunshot explodes in the air. Dad doesn't need to drag me any more. I thunder down the road with him by my side. We jump into the car as another gunshot erupts. Dad flings the car around, spinning a one-hundred-and-eighty-degree turn. The tyres screech on the road but neither of us cares. Out of the back window, through my NVGs, I see a green human shape sprinting towards us.

'Down,' yells Dad, pushing the back of my head so I fall into the footwell.

There's another gunshot. We tear down the street. My heartbeat thrashes in my ears. Dad swerves around corner after corner through the village, my body flings from side to side. I feel the car straighten up as we hit the main road but Dad doesn't slow down.

'Are they following us?' I ask.

'I don't think so,' says Dad. He drives fast for another five minutes and then pulls over to the side of the road. 'Are you OK?'

I clamber back onto my seat, my body trembling. 'That . . . that was a gun.'

'I know, I saw it through the window of our house. Now you know why I wanted you to stay in the car.'

For what feels like the hundredth time that day, I say, 'I'm sorry. I'm so sorry.'

'Scar,' says Dad, stretching out his hand, as if he's going to touch the top of my head. Then he stops, his arm hovering in the air. 'Never mind.' He puts his hand back onto the steering wheel.

I drop my head. I wanted him to tell me it was OK. I wanted him to tell me he's glad I'm safe.

'Who were they? What did they want?' I ask, quietly.

'I don't know,' says Dad. 'But to be honest, they could be any one of our targets, someone we've burgled before. They were looking for something. They were ransacking our house when they saw me.'

'They saw you?'

'They were wearing NVGs too.'

My stomach twists. Strangers rifling through our stuff. Wearing night-vision goggles like professionals. Carrying guns.

'Can we go back there?' I ask.

'I'm afraid not. The house is compromised.'

My stomach twists even more—all our stuff's back there. 'Well, when can we?'

'We can't. We're never going back.'

CHAPTER
SEVEN

I rub my eyes and sit up in bed, staring at the crumbling plaster and mould crawling up the walls. For a moment I can't work out where I am. Then the night comes flooding back. We're in one of Dad's safe houses—the Anderson. We've left home for ever.

Nausea wells in my stomach, threatening to rise to my throat. I want to close my eyes, make all of this go away, but I know I can't. And so I drag myself out of bed. My toes recoil at the cold flagstone floor.

We're in a small one-storey cottage on Dartmoor. It has five rooms—two bedrooms, a kitchen, a lounge, and a bathroom. The windows are tiny, allowing in only slivers of light, and the beamed ceilings are low. It's in the middle of a wood, in the middle of nowhere. Occasionally, an odd hiker stumbles upon it, but on the whole, nobody knows it exists.

I glance at my watch. It's one in the afternoon. Whoa—I really slept in!

'Dad!' I call, walking into the lounge.

There's no answer.

'Dad, are you awake?'

I poke my head into his room to see the bed made and his clothes from last night draped over a chair. But he isn't there.

'Dad,' I call again, heading into the kitchen.

A used mug and note lie on the counter.

Scar,

I've gone into town for money and food. There are baked beans in a pan if you're hungry. I should be back in about two hours. Please don't leave the house. If you get bored, feel free to do some cleaning.

Dad.

P.S Make sure you wear slippers. I don't want you catching a cold.

I roll my eyes at the last line. Dad lets me scale twelve-metre buildings but he's worried about a cold floor. Then I snort. He's left me on my own already. I'd kind of hoped he'd want to talk to me, reassure me about how we're never going home.

I lean over and touch the mug. It's still warm, which means he hasn't been gone too long. Since I can't be bothered to heat up the beans, I eat them lukewarm. There's an empty tin of tuna on the side too, and I guess Dad's eaten it all. He knew I wouldn't want any for I haven't touched meat or fish in five years. After showering, I squeeze into a pair of old jeans and a T-shirt that I find in my wardrobe. They're too small but they'll do until I get new ones. I'm going to have to get new everything!

Then I start to work on the house. I know Dad doesn't expect to see the cottage gleaming but I want to impress him—like a kind of apology. I tear down the cobwebs, making sure I carry the spiders to safety first. I dust every surface, mop every floor. Looking at the time, I'm startled to see that it's already been two hours. Dad will be back soon.

Two hours run into three. I pace around the lounge and look out of the window for some sign of a car. Three hours become four, and an uneasy knot begins forming in my gut. Surely it shouldn't take this long to go to the bank and get some food?

I decide I'll wait one more hour—the note *does* say not to leave the house. But if he's not home by then, I'll head into town, see if he's all right. Hugging my knees, I sit on the sofa, my eyes darting between my watch and the dirt track. Time crawls, when all of a sudden I hear a rumble.

I leap to my feet and glance through the small window expecting to see Dad's black car. My throat tightens. My legs weaken.

A black van rumbles up the dirt track. Even though the letters have disappeared, I recognize it immediately.

Parcel Deliveries. What's it doing here? How did they find out about this safe house? I stare in shock for a moment. Then instinct takes over. I race to my bedroom and grab my rucksack.

Keeping hidden at the edge of Dad's bedroom window, I peep around the curtains. A guy is standing on our driveway, staring at the house. I recognize him—the stinking delivery guy. He's not wearing a leather jacket any more, just a T-shirt. Even from over here, I can make out his arm muscles. If he grabs hold of me, I won't be able to escape.

He swaggers to the front door. I drop to my knees and crawl on all fours into the lounge, making sure I'm well below window height. There's a bang on the door and the walls of the house seem to shake.

'Scarlet, I know you're in there!' he shouts. 'It'll be easier if you let me in.'

Easier for you! I think, scrabbling across the floor. As soon as I reach the kitchen, I climb to my feet. I ease the back door open and slip outside. The trees are about twenty metres away. Although I don't have any cover, I hope the guy will concentrate on the front of the house for just a little longer. I start to sprint.

'She's back here!' someone yells.

I look over my shoulder to see a boy about my age charging towards me. He must have been scoping the back of the house. How did I not notice?

'Grab her!' yells the delivery guy, storming around the side of the house.

I race through the clearing, my heart pounding. The boy's footsteps are getting closer.

'Matt, tackle her!' bawls the delivery guy.

'But she's a girl!' yells the boy, so close to me the words pierce my ears.

'Do it!'

I can't be knocked down. I stop abruptly, spinning around, pulling back my arm. Within seconds my fist connects with the boy's face. There's a crunch and a yelp, and the boy's legs buckle. I twist back around and hurtle for the woods.

'She hit me! She freakin' hit me!' shrieks Matt.

'You should have got her first!' shouts the delivery guy.

I hear another set of footsteps—they're heavier and faster.

'Scarlet, we have your Dad! We need him to give us the bracelet.'

My legs stumble and I have to use all my strength to stop falling to the ground. They have Dad . . .

'That's right, wait for me,' yells the delivery guy.

Something inside of me screams NO! Before I know it, my legs are pounding the ground, and I'm running harder than I've ever run before.

Reaching the edge of the wood, I slalom between trees. I scramble over roots and crash through waist-high nettles and ferns. Hurtling deeper and deeper into the woods, branches scratch my skin. If only I could get out of his line of vision, I'd scale a tree and hide. A stitch scorches my side and my lungs are ready to explode. I'm getting hotter and hotter, but I can't stop. I expect his stink to reach me first, but he's obviously washed. I don't smell him at all. It's his feet I hear. He's fast. He's fit. He's closing in. There's no way my punch would damage him.

Suddenly I hear him trip. Thank God! This might be my only chance. Sweat pouring, I dart behind a thicker set of trees, searching for one to climb. Then all at once my wrist starts to burn. It's as if someone's twisting it, cutting off my blood supply. I paw at it with my other hand, trying to find the source of the pain. Nothing's there.

The delivery guy's footsteps get closer. I don't have time to climb a tree now. Trying to ignore my throbbing wrist, I run farther into the woods. Then, just as fast as it started, the pain stops. It's replaced with something else, something I've never felt before. My entire body seems to be liquefying—skin, limbs, muscles, bones—all of it melting. My head is dripping into my shoulders, my shoulders into my chest. I don't feel solid anymore. I feel like I'm sloshing through the woods. Any minute now I'll collapse into a puddle.

I want to stop running but my liquid legs and feet refuse. My vision blurs. Somehow I manage to detect a tree stump lying in my path. I leap over it . . . but my watery feet don't return to the ground. My liquid arms stretch out wide and I rise into the air.

The melting sensation stops as I swoop higher and higher. My eyes clear, but my brain can't compute what I'm seeing. I'm surging upwards, past the trunk of a tree, past the branches. I burst above the treetops into pure blue sky. The air rushes through my fingers. I can hear the guys trample through the woods and I can see the tops of their heads clearly, as they dart in and out of the trees.

I feel free, powerful. I can see for miles. With an explosion of energy I fly far away. Swooping through the air, the breeze ripples through my feathers . . .

Then my brain focuses. Feathers? What? How? My eyes flicker right. Where my fingers should be are the tips of a brown wing. *What the . . . ?* I bend my wing towards me, transfixed, and immediately drop out of the sky. I tumble through branches until I slam into the ground below.

Then there is only darkness.

CHAPTER EiGHT

My head is pounding. I force my eyes open. I'm lying on . . . grass? Everything's blurry, but it seems that the night sky is above me. Where's the ceiling? Where's my bed? I heave onto my shoulders and my head hurts even more. Reaching for my scalp, I feel something wet. Blood? I think in horror.

My eyes slowly grow used to the darkness and I realize wild ponies and sheep are staring at me. *What the . . . ?*

'Dad,' I yell.

There's no answer, and tears stab my eyes. I swipe them aside.

'Dad!' I scream at the top of my voice. This time when I hear nothing, bubbles of panic swirl inside of me. How did I get here? The last thing I remember is tidying up the Anderson house.

Closing my eyes, it all hurtles back. I was running away from those guys . . . those guys who have Dad! I went into the woods and then—I look upwards and ice shoots through my body. I came from *up there*—in the sky. With long brown wings, I soared above the treetops.

All at once I can't breathe. I gasp for air, clutch my stomach. Then I think of Dad's words. I can almost hear his voice: 'Scar, don't panic. You know it makes things worse.'

I force myself to breathe slower—in and out, in and out—and soon I have some control over my body. I shake my throbbing head. What is wrong with me? I'm hallucinating about birds.

And right now I don't have time to worry about it. Those guys think Dad has the bracelet—but he doesn't. What will they do to him when they realize? Then my heart stops. In my mind I see a white medicine box on the kitchen counter. Dad's insulin. He doesn't have it. He takes it once a week, so he'll need it on Friday. Today is—oh God what day is it? My head feels so woozy. Scrunching my eyes, I try to think. Today is Wednesday. Very early Wednesday.

I have three days to find him.

First things first though—where the hell am I?

Ignoring my pounding head, I clamber to my feet. By the looks of the wild ponies, long dry grasses, and desolate trees, I must still be on Dartmoor. There are a few scattered lights in the valley below of a town or village. If I head there, I 'll be able to work out where I am, and then I can start looking for Dad. Although how, I'm not exactly sure.

With a sense of purpose, I step forwards, when my toes hit something soft. Looking down, I discover my rucksack lying at my feet. How did that get there? I thought I'd lost it back in the woods when . . . I shake my head. I'm not going to think about that.

Hoisting my bag onto my shoulder, I storm down the hill. Ponies and sheep scatter. Even though I moved quickly, the sky is turning blue by the time I leave the fields and hit the main road. My head hurts and my feet ache, but I refuse to slow down. If anything I speed up as I reach a sign welcoming me to Bucklandleigh. Dad and I have passed this sign many times on the way to the Anderson, which means I was right. I am still on Dartmoor.

I enter an old English town, with crooked thatched roof cottages, bunting, and quaint little shops. It's the sort of place Mum would have loved. She'd have bought me cake and juice at a teashop. A couple of elderly dog walk-ers head towards me. I smile blandly, but their jaws drop, as they look me up and down.

Do I really look that bad?

Walking hurriedly past, I dart into a side street. Then I stop. My hands grow clammy, as I stare into the shop window. It's full of computers and laptops . . . like Dad's laptop hidden inside the fireplace. Surely the burglars won't have found that. If I can get home, I'll be able to find out who Dad's clients are, where they live. Then I'll be able to find out who wanted the bracelet.

I start to look at the cars parked on the side of the road—I need one without an alarm—when suddenly I hear wheels turning on some tracks. They slow down, and within seconds, I'm running, following the noise. Racing down street after street, finally I see it. A railway station. Who knew getting home would be this easy?

I charge onto the one and only platform, just as a train powers away. The place is completely empty. There isn't even a person selling tickets, just an electronic machine. Fortunately the timetables are plastered to a wall, and I scan them, searching for a train to Crewkerne, the nearest station to my village. Then my heart plummets. There isn't another train in that direction for at least seven hours. The train I heard rush past was the one I should have caught.

I glare at the empty platform. Have I really got to wait here all day? I can't. I need to get to the laptop, to Dad. I sigh heavily. I'm going to have to hotwire a car after all.

Twisting around, I step towards the exit, when a yellow sandwich board catches my eye.

Written in bright red letters are the words, *Visit the British Museum in London. See the Greek, Egyptian, and Aztec exhibitions. Discover their legends.*

Below the words are three pictures. I hardly look at the first two—a sculpture of a Greek god and an Egyptian mummy. But I can't take my eyes off the third. It's a bracelet—a gold bracelet with turquoise creatures running around the outside. I look at my left wrist and swallow. Then all at once my wrist starts to tingle as if it's trying to tell me something. I don't understand why, but somehow I know I have to go to London.

'But what about Dad?' shrieks a voice inside my head.

I have to get his insulin to him in three days. I should be trying to get home. But what if home is being watched? I gnaw on my lip, when my wrist tingles again. I'm decided. London first. Then Dad.

Now—I just have to find a way to sneak on board a train.

CHAPTER NINE

I feel like I made the right decision, since the next train to London is due in ten minutes. I pace the platform, willing the train to get here faster, when I notice a laminated 'Out of Order' sign stuck to the outside of a toilet door. I look around. Good—the platform is still empty. Peeling the sign off the door, I shove it into my rucksack, before stripping off the Blu-tack too. On the way back to the centre of the platform, I grab a map of London from a stand.

The train arrives on time and I get on at the front, where a few passengers in suits are reading newspapers. I wander towards the back of the train, stopping just before the last carriage. There are two toilets in this section, on opposite sides. I pull the sign out of my rucksack and stick it to one of the doors using the Blu-tack. Then I slide inside and lock the door.

OK—it isn't the most comfortable of rooms but hopefully I can stay here, undisturbed. More importantly, I won't be charged for a fare.

I put my rucksack down on the floor and look in the mirror above the sink. My mouth drops. No wonder those dog walkers stared at me. My clothes are ripped and muddy. My hair is matted with blood and I have a thick scar crawling across my cheek like a caterpillar. I look like I've been thrown through a car window. I'm used to blending into the background, but looking like this, I might as well have a flashing neon sign over my head.

I lean over the sink and scrub my skin, hair, clothes. I manage to make my face look slightly better but I can't get the stains out of my jeans and T-shirt. Now they're not only filthy and ripped, they're cold and wet too. After a while I give up. I'll find some new clothes in London. A hoodie would be good.

Flopping onto the toilet lid, I open out the map of London. Water drips off my hair onto my shoulders, as I work out a route on foot to the British Museum. It's further than I would like, but I can't risk taking an underground train. Security on the London Tube is far too tricky to bypass. I stuff the map into my back pocket.

The train keeps stopping, much to my annoyance. On occasions, I hear passengers grunt outside my door, probably at the sight of the sign, but nobody tries to open it. At some point I must fall asleep, because I wake up to find my face lying on a toilet roll. A bored voice talking into a loudspeaker informs me we are arriving at London

58

Waterloo. I sit up and wipe my face. Mr Anchor was right. I do drool.

At last the train stops and I hear crowds of people getting off, but still I wait. When I haven't heard anything for a while, I open the door a fraction, and peer outside. To my relief, the train is empty. I pull the 'Out of Order' sign and Blu-tack off the door and roll them up, before stuffing them into my bag. Then I step out onto the platform.

It's heaving. There are ticket collectors everywhere, guarding the turnstiles. I need a distraction. I wait a moment to see if anything happens. Nothing. OK—I need to *cause* a distraction.

An elderly woman is nearby, checking her bag.

'Oh God,' I gasp in a loud whisper. 'Someone's fallen on the track.'

'Someone's fallen on the track?' she cries, looking in my direction.

I dart behind a pillar as other travellers start to shout, 'Someone's on the track.'

Within seconds, passengers, guards, children are rushing towards the railway line. No one's looking at the turnstile behind the pillar. I grab onto it and swing my legs over. My feet land on the other side and I glance around. Phew—no one's noticed. They're too busy looking for the fallen passenger.

I dart into the crowd and wander through the station. Some people's eyes widen when they see me, but thankfully I'm not stopped.

I keep my head down and hurry towards the River Thames. I want to rush through the South Bank too—a promenade filled with cafes, restaurants, and street entertainers—but it's too crowded. I have to slow down.

I walk past a French restaurant so crowded the tables are spilling onto the promenade. The smells of food are agony. I'm just thinking about swiping a baguette off someone's plate when two loud voices catch my attention.

'You asked me to buy you some jeans so that is what I did.'

'I wanted red ones. Not blue.'

I locate the voices. A woman with perfectly coiffed golden hair glowers at her daughter. The girl is about my size, possibly a little taller. They're sitting at a table a metre or so away from the menu-covered sandwich board. Walking over, I pretend to examine it.

'The shop assistant said everyone is wearing the blue,' says the mother, clutching a large white bag with the name Charcoal broadcast on the side.

My eyes hone in on the bag. So these clothes aren't wanted . . .

'Exactly,' says the girl, not even bothering to look up from the mobile phone she's playing on. 'I don't want to be like everyone else.'

'I even got you a top to go with them,' says the mother.

'Take them back.'

'I am not going all the way back to Charcoal just because you don't like blue.'

'I won't wear them,' says the girl. She looks up and smiles spitefully. 'Dad would have bought me the red ones.'

'Then your dad can,' hisses the mother, shoving the bag down at the base of her chair.

Can I just walk past and grab it? I wonder.

The woman lifts her head sideways and shouts, 'Waiter, I'd like the bill please.'

Both the girl and mother look towards a waiter who's delivering drinks to a table near the entrance of the indoor section of the restaurant. I take a step closer to the bag.

'I said, Waiter, I'd like the bill, please,' says the woman, louder this time.

'Mum, he's busy with someone else. Wait a minute.'

'Waiter!' barks the woman.

The waiter turns and the bottled water tips. He tries to grab them but he's too late. They crash to the floor. Water sprays everywhere. Customers scream and everyone turns to face the noise.

Talk about being given a chance! I stroll past their table, bend down to scratch my ankle, and pluck the Charcoal bag off the floor. Within seconds I'm walking away.

'That was your fault,' says the girl to her mother. 'You made him jump.'

'Don't you dare blame me. You blame me for everything!'

Their words trail into the distance as I merge back into the crowds of people along the South Bank. Now I can get changed. But I have to be quick.

Darting into a busy café, I head straight for the toilets. Ripping off the price tags, I change in record time. The top doesn't have a hood and is sparklier than I would like, but the jeans fit perfectly. I silently thank the woman with coiffed hair for buying blue. They look like every other pair of jeans I've ever owned.

I hurry out of the café, and stuff my old clothes into a bin, before heading for a bridge over the river. It's only when I reach the other side that I remember the map of London. For a moment I consider turning back to get it from the bin. But that would take too much time. I've wasted enough already. Instead I close my eyes and visualize the route in my head. No, I don't need the map.

It takes a further thirty minutes, darting through the streets of London, past restaurants, cafes, clothes shops, and the most gimmicky tourist shops I've ever seen. Does anyone actually buy sequinned union-jack top hats or beach towels with the royal family on them?

At last I arrive at the cast iron railings surrounding the British Museum. My palms grow sweaty. Am I about to learn the secrets of the bracelet? More importantly, am I about to discover what on earth is happening to me?

CHAPTER
TEN

Walking into the British Museum, my whole body's on edge. A giant stone head from Easter Island greets me, and I glower at it. Surely it should still be on Easter Island instead of here? Then I press it to the back of my mind. Dad and the bracelet are all that's important now.

According to a map on the wall, the Aztec exhibition is on the ground floor. I push through a set of glass double doors and find the Americas rooms. Yet these exhibits are too modern. I need ancient America.

Walking faster, I turn down a corridor, straight into a large group of French children, about the same age as me. They're blocking the hall, laughing, chewing gum, taking pictures of each other. I want to barge through them, but that will attract attention. Instead I say, 'Excuse me.'

No one gets out of my way.

Through gritted teeth, I say, '*Excusez moi.*'

Still no one moves. One girl blows a bubble in my face and the others laugh. My fists instinctively clench and I feel my face tense up. The girl's eyes widen and she leaps out of my way. Gasps fly from the mouths of the rest of the party as they move to the sides, leaving a pathway down the middle. Why are they suddenly letting me through?

I eye each one of them warily as I make my way down the corridor. They look . . . scared? I push through another set of glass double doors. As soon as the doors swing back to their closed position, the babble of French begins again, but I can't understand a word they're saying.

I walk further into the room when I catch a glimpse of my reflection in the glass of a cabinet. *What the . . . ?*

I have fangs: long, sharp, daggers dripping over my bottom lip as if I'm a vampire. Then, in front of my eyes, the fangs recede. I stare at my reflection for a moment longer, waiting for my teeth to grow or shrink or do something, anything. Nothing happens.

I shake my head in disbelief. Then all at once, I spy something towards the back of the room and I forget about my teeth. An enormous glass cabinet is split into three sections. Halfway up the left compartment is a terrifying mask —black mosaic with a turquoise nose, sharp fangs, and wide oval holes for eyes. As if in a trance I walk towards it, barely aware of the tablets to my left and sculptures to my right.

Straight away I know this mask is Aztec. It's too similar to the one Dad and I stole to be anything else. Does it belong to the descendent of the Aztec priest too? But even if it does, I know we'll never steal it back for him. Dad will never steal from a museum or charity.

My wrist starts to tingle and I place my hand flat against the glass counter.

'Beautiful, isn't it?' says a voice, yanking me back to the real world. 'It's a new acquisition.'

I spin around to see a short, round, bald-headed man grinning at me. He wears a badge telling me he works at the museum and that his name is Mr Tomlinson.

'I wouldn't say beautiful. Ugly and terrifying maybe.'

Mr Tomlinson grins even more. 'Well, it's supposed to be. It's a wolf mask. An Aztec warrior would wear it into battle, terrifying his enemies.'

My wrist tingles again and my eyes sweep over the rest of the exhibits. There are large stone sculptures of gods, mosaic helmets, and ceremonial shields, but there's no sign of any jewellery. I frown.

'Are you looking for something in particular?' asks Mr Tomlinson.

'I . . . I don't suppose you know anything about a gold bracelet?' I say. 'It's got turquoise stones on it. I saw a picture of it at the railway station and—'

'Ah! You mean the bracelet of Achcauhtli,' says Mr Tomlinson.

My stomach somersaults. 'I do?'

'Come with me.'

Turning to follow him, I spot a girl on the other side of the glass double doors I came through. She's the French girl I frightened earlier, and she's talking to a grown-up. They both look around and my spine tingles. Are they looking for me? But why? What I saw in my reflection couldn't be true . . .

Ducking to hide my face, I follow Mr Tomlinson. He squeezes his rather large frame behind the cabinet and leads me into a smaller room. If he hadn't shown me, I wouldn't have known this room was here. Hopefully the French girl won't either.

Shaking the girl from my mind, I look at what Mr Tomlinson's pointing to—a tapestry hanging within a large glass picture frame. My mouth grows drier than sandpaper. The tapestry is about one and half metres long and one metre high, the background woven in fabrics of green and purple. In the centre, woven from sparkling gold, is a picture of a bracelet. Turquoise creatures run around the outside of the golden band. Instantly I recognize the bird with long wings, and now that the images are larger, I can make out a lizard and a wildcat too. The other two shapes remain unclear.

'Have you ever seen the real thing?' I ask, breathlessly.

'The bracelet? No one has,' says Mr Tomlinson. 'It doesn't exist.'

'What?' I jerk round to look at him. 'What do you mean it doesn't exist?'

'Many historians and archaeologists have spent years—and I mean *years*—searching for such a piece, but to no avail. This is what we think it would have looked like, though.' He steps aside to reveal a gold bracelet sitting inside a glass box.

I want to yell, 'That's wrong!' But I keep my mouth shut. The gold is in one solid piece instead of created from woven interlinked threads. And the turquoise stones have been carved far too perfectly, not abstract enough. In fact, looking at these stones, I can make out the last two creatures. A monkey? A dog?

'Are you all right? That's quite a scowl,' says Mr Tomlinson.

I try to clear my face. 'The poster said there was a legend attached to this bracelet. Do you know what it is?'

'Oh yes, it's one of my favourite stories.'

French voices drift into the main room. My heart begins to pound. Are they the party from earlier? If so, let them just be interested in the exhibition. And don't let them find this room!

'Have you ever heard of a Nahualli?' he asks.

'A Na—what?' I say, stealing a nervous glance to the open doorway.

'A Nahualli. It's an Aztec word, meaning "shadow soul." It's your animal twin, your spirit double. Born at the same time as you, you share each other's souls.' Mr Tomlinson clasps his hands together. 'Aztecs believed animals lived on this world with the gods long before any human was born. Therefore animals are sacred. They should be respected and listened to. Never dominated or mistreated.'

Now that I agree with!

'Usually the Nahualli has traits that reflect those of the person they belong to. If you are clever and curious your Nahualli might be the monkey. If you have courage and search for perspective it might be the eagle.'

My scalp prickles.

'You should nurture your Nahualli and in return it will give you guidance, teach you skills and secrets. For the normal man, the Nahualli was a spirit that would come to you in dreams. Or sometimes if you were lucky, it would appear to you in the real world.'

'You sound as if you believe this,' I say, my eyes still darting back and forth to the doorway.

'I've spent years studying it at university. Sometimes I wish it were true.'

The French voices become louder. Then I hear someone in English say, 'Fangs?'

'*Oui!*' shouts a chorus of children.

Oh God! Did I really grow them? No, I couldn't have!

I should get out of here, but I have to know the story. 'Mr Tomlinson, you said there was a legend,' I whisper.

'Maybe I should tell it to you in the main room. There seems to be a lot of people out there.'

'No!' I snap.

Mr Tomlinson looks startled.

'If—if you don't mind I would love to hear it in here . . . where . . . I can see the bracelet.'

'I fully understand,' he says, beaming again. 'Back in the fifteen hundreds, there was a Spanish conquistador, Cortez,

68

who invaded Mexico on behalf of the king of Spain. He and his men killed many Aztecs, stealing their possessions, their land. Unsurprisingly the Aztecs were outraged. So much so, five high priests of Mexico came together. Now the high priests had extraordinary relationships with their Nahuallis. They worked hard to gain control over their spiritual twins until eventually they learnt how to transform into them.'

I drop my rucksack, and no longer care about the French babble outside. 'They . . . they could transform into an animal?'

'Yes. I know it sounds ridiculous to us, but that was their belief. Each high priest changed into a different creature. The highest of all high priests, Achcauhtli, changed into a jaguar.'

'The wildcat on the bracelet?'

'Very good,' says Mr Tomlinson, nodding.

'So . . . by the turquoise on the bracelet, I'm guessing there was a bird Nahualli?' My voice quivers.

'Yes, an eagle.'

A bark of nervous laughter escapes my lips.

Mr Tomlinson looks carefully at me. 'Are you all right? You look white as a sheet!'

'I'm fine,' I say, wrapping my arms around my body. 'So the bracelet represents the priests and their Nahuallis?'

'Yes. But there is much more to this story.' says Mr Tomlinson. 'The high priests went to the temple of their god, Tezcatlipoca. They cut through their skin, spilled their blood, and mixed it with melted gold. From the mixture, they weaved a bracelet, and added turquoise stones. Under Tezcatlipoca's orders, Achcauhtli put the bracelet on and it sucked straight into his bloodstream.'

I gulp and stare at my wrist.

'It's a horrific thought, isn't it? Something sucking into your bloodstream?'

I nod slowly.

'From that moment on, Achcauhtli could transform into any of the five animals, depending on what power he needed.'

'Five? What were they?' I whisper.

'The jaguar, the monkey, the eagle, the wolf, and the alligator.'

An eagle with long brown wings. A jaguar with long fangs and sharp claws. The world seems to spin and I feel dizzy. I lean against a cabinet for support.

'Oh—would you mind not leaning on that please?' says Mr Tomlinson. 'I wouldn't want the powder to spill.'

Still dazed, I turn to look at the cabinet I was resting against. It only has one thing in it—a brown woven sack the size of my hand. It's open slightly, filled with yellow powder. Its label says: '*pahtli teilnamiquilizpatlaloni*'. The translation underneath says, 'an instrument for changing people's memories'.

'It's supposed to be a powerful magic,' says Mr Tomlinson. 'When someone's sleeping or knocked out, you take a pinch and place it on their tongue. The powder sizzles and you speak aloud, telling that person what you want them to forget and what you want them to remember.'

It looks like crushed sand to me, I think.

Then suddenly a face appears in the doorway. I swallow hard. The French girl from earlier. She's found this room. More importantly, she's found me.

'*C'est pour elle*,' she shouts, pointing at me. '*La petite fille avec les crocs!*'

More faces arrive, nodding and shouting, when a woman pushes her way through the group.

I step backwards.

'Excuse me,' says the woman to Mr Tomlinson, with a thick French accent. 'This girl has been scaring my pupils.'

I try to act as if I don't know what she's talking about. I shrug, but inside I feel my body grow hot. The room, the people—they're closing in. I glance up at Mr Tomlinson. He's looking at me strangely. I need air . . . now!

I barge through the doorway. The French party springs out of my way.

'Wait!' shouts Mr Tomlinson.

Looking over my shoulder, I croak, 'Thanks for the history lesson.'

'Hang on,' he shouts and to my horror, he starts to follow.

My walk turns into a run. Dodging displays and visitors, I hurtle through the museum. As I reach the exit I steal a glimpse behind. You're kidding! Mr Tomlinson is still chasing me. He's fast for his size.

Then he waves a rucksack in the air. 'Your bag!' he splutters.

My heart jumps, and I spin around. I touch my shoulder just to check he hasn't got an exact replica in his hand. Nope—he's got my rucksack with the tools inside. How could I have let that out of my grasp?

Sprinting back, I take the rucksack from him. 'Thanks, that was really kind of you.'

'You're welcome,' he gasps in between wheezes.

He bends down, clutching his stomach, and I spot the French party coming our way. My heart pounds again.

'Err—thank you,' I say.

I bolt out of the museum, and run down numerous roads. Glancing behind, to my relief, no one's following. Finally I can stop. Leaning against a wall, my head spins. Is it possible that Achcauhtli's bracelet has sucked into my bloodstream? Have I transformed into an eagle? Have my teeth and fingernails grown? Or were they all hallucinations? I slam my head against the stone. I must be going mad if I'm even asking these questions. I thought going to the museum was going to help me, but in reality it's making me lose my mind!

But I can't stay here. I have to get to Dad.

I drag myself away from the wall and start heading for Waterloo once more. I want to forget about the legend. I want to concentrate on getting to that laptop. For I will find out who ordered the bracelet. And then . . .

Then what?

Who am I kidding? I'm just a girl going against professionals with guns and NVGs. They're probably waiting for me at home right now. Fear ripples through me and

I'm tempted to stop again, but somehow I manage to keep moving. Why couldn't I have been kidnapped instead of Dad? He'd know what to do.

In fact—he'd have rescued me by now!

CHAPTER ELEVEN

In a kind of trance, I make it to the railway station. I find a train that's leaving in twenty minutes and sneak aboard. No one's near a toilet in the middle of the train so I slap the 'Out of Order' sign onto the door. I settle into the small cubicle, knowing I'm going to be here for a while, and try to fall asleep. But Mr Tomlinson's words ring in my ears and I can't stop thinking of long brown wings and sharp teeth.

The journey seems to be endless when at last the bored voice over the loud speaker announces we're nearing Crewkerne. I let out a silent sigh, and climb to my feet, when footsteps approach the cubicle.

'I don't believe this—the toilet's out of order again,' says a woman. 'What's wrong with it?'

'I don't know,' replies another female voice. 'I don't particularly want to find out.'

I wait for them to walk away, choose another toilet, but instead the door rattles. They're trying to open the door. At the same time, the train starts slowing down.

Oh no! I can't reach my stop yet, not with these women hovering outside.

'It's locked,' says the first woman.

'That's because it's out of order.'

'It's locked from the inside,' she snaps. 'I think some-one's hiding in there, dodging the fare.'

You have got to be kidding! Not now!

'Maybe someone is on the toilet and hasn't noticed the sign,' says the second woman.

'I hope not. You're not allowed to use the toilet in a station.' There's a loud bang on the door. 'I know you're in there!' she shouts.

I don't say a word.

'He's hiding!' she snaps, banging the door even harder. 'You won't get away with this. I'll wait here all day if I have to.'

My fists open and close. Go away!

'I'm going to take you straight to the police station,' she shouts.

The police station? That's the one place I really can't go. I stare at the closed door, my brain going wild, trying to work out what to do. I feel hot. Sweat drips down my back. Then all of a sudden my wrist hurts, as if some invisible force is strangling it. The pain tightens. I want to scream but I can't let those women know I'm here. Instead I clench my jaw but I can't even do that for long.

My body starts to liquefy. My head dissolves into my neck. Then all at once the ceiling looks further away and the walls close in, like someone has grabbed hold of the cubicle and stretched it.

I feel strong. Powerful. Not scared of anything.

'I don't think anyone's in there. We should leave,' says the second woman, her voice sounding louder and clearer than before.

'No, he's committing a crime. He should be punished.'

If they're planning on sending me to the police station they deserve to pay. I open my mouth and roar.

'What was that?' shrieks the second woman.

I swipe the lock and the door springs open. Two women in railway uniforms leap back, their eyes white with fear. I snarl, and lean back on my haunches, ready to pounce, ready to rip out their—

What am I thinking? I force my body to twist around and run through the carriage.

People scream and scramble to the sides of the train, flattening themselves against the windows. An alarm screeches out as someone hits the emergency stop button. The train squeals to a halt and I charge through a second carriage when I sniff something. Something delicious. I'm so hungry. I want food. I *need* food.

I stop and turn my head. A man sits frozen in a seat, his bacon baguette hovering in his hand just in front of his face. I lick my lips and droplets of saliva fall to the floor. Lifting back my head, I roar. The man drops his baguette and I snatch it in my teeth before it reaches his lap.

I spin around, searching for more to eat. The screams grow louder. Then the train doors open. I race through the rest of the carriage and leap out. Fresh air swoops through my fur as I run faster and faster. I leap off the end of the platform, my claws scraping the gravel of the railway tracks before they hit soft grass. I race through farmland, the shouts behind me vanishing in the wind.

I jump over a hedge straight into a field of sheep. My hunger grows. I head straight for the smallest, the weakest, craving the taste. Within seconds, the lamb is clamped between my teeth, squirming as I bite down.

What am I doing? Stop!

I freeze.

Let go!

My stomach and mind seem to be wrestling.

Now!

I open my mouth and the lamb drops to the floor, wet with slobber. It clambers to its feet and limps away. I feel sick with shame, with horror. What is happening to me? Am I so hungry I'm willing to kill?

Before my stomach can win over my mind, I charge through the field, not looking at anything with a heartbeat. I need to get far away from here. I need to get home. Keeping to the shadows of hedges and trees, I head straight to our village. I run along a back road hardly used by anyone and pass the entrance to a long sweeping driveway, minutes from my house. I stumble. For on the opposite side of the drive is a roadside mirror, and I just glimpsed something…something that I can't explain. I turn back round and walk towards it.

A coldness hits my core. Prowling towards the mirror is a wildcat with wild eyes. A jaguar. I blink. The jaguar blinks. Standing directly in front of the glass, my brain seems to fog and defog at the same time. I turn my head. The reflection turns its head.

My insides squirm. Suddenly I feel like my limbs are melting, my muscles turning to liquid. Right before my eyes, the fur sucks back into my body. My skin bubbles, like porridge boiling in a pan. If I wasn't so fascinated, I'd be sick. I automatically lean backwards onto two legs. The claws on my paws recoil. Mousy hair sprouts and my clothes reappear, faint at first, but then the colours grow stronger, brighter. My brown eyes turn grey. My fangs recede. A rucksack emerges on my shoulder. My skin becomes smooth, apart from the scar on my cheek, and I am a girl once more.

Oh God!

Wrapping my arms around my body, I stare at the ashen-faced girl in the mirror. I gasp for air. My body shakes. How did this happen? Things like this don't happen—it's impossible. Then Mr Tomlinson's words chime in my ear. Achcauhtli transformed into five animals. Well . . . I just changed into a jaguar and most likely an eagle before that. I bite back a scream. Does this mean I can change into three other creatures as well?

Staggering over to a grassy bank, I fall to the ground. I bend my knees, clutch my legs and rock back and forth. Somewhere deep down, I realize I've known this all along. Gold doesn't dissolve through old age. I didn't escape those men by running. The powers of that bracelet, of the five high priests, are inside me. Somehow I can change into animals—into Nahuallis! And those Nahuallis carry out my deepest desires. If I need to escape, they fly away. If I'm angry, they attack. If I'm hungry, they search for food at any cost.

I'm not sure how long I sit on the grass, rocking like a madman, but finally I decide to stop. Now is not the time for self-pity or fear. Now is the time for action. I have to find Dad.

I clamber to my feet—luckily no one is about—and grip my rucksack. I race along the back road until I reach the woods behind our home, where I become slower and quieter. My heart is pounding so loudly I'm sure if the burglars are still there, they'll hear me. I stand behind a tree at the edge of the garden and look towards the house. There are no signs of movement.

I run softly around the edge of the garden and see the lounge window has been smashed. The burglars weren't that professional, then! Crouching, I make my way along the back wall of the house until I'm beneath the broken window. I listen for footsteps or talking, but I can't hear a thing. Are they hiding somewhere?

Slowly I stand and peer into the lounge. Heat flushes through my body. I clench my jaws. Books have been thrown from the shelves, pictures torn off the walls, sofas turned upside down. The gold mirror from above the mantelpiece lies in pieces on the floor. But as I look at the fireplace, my jaws unclench. The log burner is in the exact same spot Dad and I left it, which means the laptop should be just where we left it.

Avoiding fragments of broken glass, I put my hands on the windowsill and swing my legs into the room. I wait to see if anyone appears. Again there's silence. Surely the burglars have gone. Dodging broken lampshades and pictures, I make my way over to the log burner. I grab the bottom rim with my fingers and heave as hard as I can. It refuses to budge. I try again, but the log burner is just too heavy.

I think about kicking it, when an uneasy thought occurs to me. I glance down at my wrist. Is it possible to use the bracelet to my advantage? Could I transform into the alligator and use its powerful jaws to drag the log burner away?

I close my eyes, and think of the giant beast. I wait for a strangling sensation to squeeze my wrist. I wait for my limbs to liquefy. But nothing. And when I open my eyes I still have two human legs, two human arms.

One thing is for certain—I have no control over these powers.

I snarl at the log burner. I need someone to help me move it. But who? Dad is the only person I trust. I think of the girls at school but I don't know where any of them live. I don't even have their phone numbers. Jules and

Charlie's numbers pop into my brain, and I'm surprised I even remember them. But I can't call. What would I say? 'I'm sorry, I've actually been lying to you for the last year. I still live in England.' Plus they live too far away. My throat thickens as I realize I'm all alone.

Oh come on, think, I tell myself. *There must be someone.*

I suppose I know our neighbours a little. But they're too old and frail . . . except . . . a flash of blond hair springs to mind.

Not only does he live nearby, he's probably as strong as me. I step forward and hesitate. Is it too risky, asking him for help? But when I look at the chaos around the room and think of Dad—wherever he is—I grimace and step forward once more.

CHAPTER TWELVE

I reach number four's garden, and the television's blaring. So I'm not surprised when I ring the bell and no one answers. I doubt anyone heard it. Plus Ethan might not even be at home. I glance up at his bedroom window; there's only one way to find out.

Running over to the large oak tree in the garden, I start climbing. The branches feel familiar and in no time at all I swing up to a bough overhanging Ethan's window. I peer inside and almost topple out of the tree. Somehow I manage to hold on.

Ethan's in there—I can see the back of his head as he plays on his computer—but he's not alone. A blonde girl sits next to him. Thank God she also has her back to me.

I release my grip, dropping to the branch below, and frown. It hadn't occurred to me someone else would be in there. *Now* who can I ask for help? With a shrinking heart, I slink down the tree and make my way across Mrs Riley's garden.

'Scarlet, are you all right?' calls a voice.

Startled, I whirl around.

Ethan is hanging out of his bedroom window, and this time there isn't just one girl, but two girls on either side of him. They're draped over his windowsill and I recognize them from school—Amanda and Louise.

'I'm fine,' I say.

'What were you doing up my tree?' asks Ethan.

'I was looking for your cat,' I say, weakly. It sounds a poor excuse even to me.

'No, you weren't,' says Amanda, shaking her long brown curls. She's the girl I didn't notice earlier. She must have been sitting somewhere else, not at his computer. 'You were looking into his room. You were spying on him.'

'No, I wasn't!' I look up at Ethan. 'I really wasn't. If you must know, I wanted to see you about something. I tried ringing your doorbell but you didn't hear. Anyway it doesn't matter now,' I add, before turning around.

'Hey, wait up,' calls Ethan.

'It really doesn't matter,' I call over my shoulder.

I jump over a hedge into the road. How could I have been so careless? Dad wouldn't be impressed.

'Scarlet, wait,' shouts Ethan. I turn around to see him running towards me, the two girls following closely behind. I stop, not wanting any of them nearer to my house than they have to be.

'What have you done to your face?' asks Ethan.

'My face?' I reach for my cheek and feel the jagged scar. I'd forgotten about that. 'I scratched it.'

'It looks deep,' says Ethan.

'Do you want a plaster?' says Louise, reaching into her bag. 'I think I've got one.'

'No!' I snap. A look of hurt crosses her face and so in a softer voice, I say, 'But thanks for asking, Louise.'

'Oh? You know my name,' she says, sounding surprised.

My stomach drops. That was careless . . . again.

'How do you know my name?' she asks.

I hesitate. 'You go to my school. You both do.' I say, finally.

'We do?' says Louise. 'I don't think I've ever seen you before.'

'I only joined last year and you're in the year above. I guess you don't notice people younger than you.'

'I guess,' says Louise, with a shrug.

Ethan's eyes dart between the three of us. 'How can you not know each other if you go to the same school?'

Because I like being invisible! But as I watch both girls eye me up and down, I realize my anonymity is gone. They'll recognize me from now on.

'So what did you want me for, anyway?' Ethan asks.

I wave my hand dismissively. 'Oh—it's nothing. I just wanted you to help me with something, but you're obviously busy. Don't worry about it.'

'I can help you now,' says Ethan.

Amanda's lips purse.

'I was only showing them how to download some films from a website,' he adds.

'Oh my God!' squeals Louise suddenly. She's staring at my legs.

'What?' I yelp, looking down. I'm not transforming into something, am I?

'I'm loving your jeans,' she cries. 'I've wanted some for ages but there's like this huge waiting list. Where did you get them?'

My jeans? You're loving my jeans? 'I . . . I just picked them up somewhere.'

'You just picked them up. They're like nine hundred pounds each,' says Louise.

They are?

'You know, I'm having a party tomorrow night,' she continues. 'My parents are going out. You could come. Ethan's coming.'

'We could go together,' he says.

Have I honestly just been invited to a party? I haven't had an invitation like this for over a year. I could go . . . have fun . . . Then I think of Dad and my chest tightens. How could I even think of such a thing? 'That's all right, I'm busy,' I say.

'How can you be too busy for a party?' says Louise.

Amanda folds her arms. 'If she says she's busy, she's busy. And Ethan, you said you were going to take me.'

'Well . . . can't we all go together?' he says. 'It would be fun.'

Amanda looks horrified by the idea.

I shake my head. 'No, really, I am too busy. But . . . thanks.' There's an awkward pause until I say, 'Well, I guess I'll leave you three to it.'

'Actually,' says Louise, linking her arm into Amanda's, 'we've got to go. I promised Mum I'd be home half an hour ago. Ethan, thanks for showing us the website. That was really cool. We'll see you tomorrow.' Her eyes flicker to my jeans. 'I hope to see you too, Scarlet.'

My stomach drops again. So now she knows my name. And it's all Ethan's fault! OK, maybe I'm being a little unfair. He wasn't expecting me. Plus he has no way of knowing my need for secrecy. But I still can't stop seething as I stand next to him, watching Louise drag Amanda away.

'You make friends quickly,' I say, through gritted teeth.

'I had to. The neighbours weren't that welcoming.'

I look at him sharply, expecting to see a cross expression, but he's grinning and there's a definite twinkle in his eye.

'So, you need my help. What can I do for you?'

I don't say anything. I don't want his help. I don't need his help . . . except I do need his help.

'You might as well tell me. I've got nothing else to do now they've gone.'

I chew my lip. 'All right,' I say, slowly, as if I'm doing him the favour. 'Can you help me lift something? It shouldn't take long.'

And then you can leave me alone. For ever.

CHAPTER THIRTEEN

I lead Ethan to the front of my house and open the door. I walk inside, careful not to step on any glass.

Ethan follows me in, and then stops, his eyes widening in horror. 'What's happened?'

'Oh . . . this,' I say. 'I hoped you wouldn't notice.'

'Wouldn't notice?' he splutters. 'You've been burgled. Have you called the police?'

'Dad has. He's with them now at the police station. That's why he couldn't help me, and I need you.'

'Your pictures are all over the floor,' says Ethan.

'Yeah. Don't stand on the broken glass.'

I steer him into the lounge, and once again he stops in the doorway.

'They've completely destroyed your house,' he says.

Seeing the devastation through his eyes seems to

make it even worse. I clench my fists so tightly, my nails cut into my palms.

'Oh God!' says Ethan. 'I should go back and warn Gran there are burglars in this area.'

'No! No, you don't need to,' I say. For as I look around the room, it dawns on me who did this. That's why they wanted the specific date. The delivery guy and whoever he works for got us to steal the double-headed serpent so we'd be out of the house. Then they could search for the bracelet. 'We were targeted,' I say flatly.

I march over to the log burner and grab the base at one end. 'Can you help me move this?'

Ethan's brow furrows as he walks towards me. 'We can't move that. It's too heavy.'

'Yes we can—it's fake. It's just too heavy for me to move on my own.'

Ethan shakes his head in disbelief but grasps hold of the other end.

'Are you ready? One . . . two . . . three.'

The log burner slides away from the hearth and I let go. Ethan doesn't move. He doesn't even untwine his fingers from the base of the log burner.

'Why do you have a fake fireplace? Why would anyone have a fake fireplace?'

Ignoring his questions, I clamber into the place where the log burner was. I stand up straight and groan. I forgot the torch! Stepping out from under the chimney, I find Ethan still looking at me, except now he's looking at me as if I've grown two heads.

'What were you doing in there?' he asks.

'I need a torch from my room. I'll be back in a sec.'

I charge up the stairs and burst through the door. I freeze. I try to swallow but I can't. I don't know why it hadn't occurred to me earlier . . . but I hadn't thought for one minute that the burglars would attack my room. They've left no drawer, no shelf untouched. My books, clothes, bedding are sprawled across the floor. My weights and broken mirror lie scattered on the carpet. My desk and bedside table are upside down.

I lift back my head and growl silently.

Ethan steps inside, and curses. 'Look what they've done to your room!'

I am looking, I think murderously. Then I see it. The glass is smashed. The frame is broken. The picture of Mum lies desolate on the floor. My heart thumps faster than ever before. My body grows hot and the strangling sensation grips my wrist. Oh no! I know what's happening.

'Ethan,' I hiss. 'Get out of here. Go back to your house.'

'No way! I'm not leaving you here on your own.'

'Ethan, I need you to go now.' My hands crash into his chest and I shove him into the hallway. Slamming the door behind him, I swiftly lock it. My muscles and limbs melt. I lean back my head and roar. I feel powerful, strong . . . and angry . . .

'Scarlet!' cries Ethan.

Instinctively I pace the carpet, stepping over broken glass, a torch, clothes. How dare strangers come in here?

How dare strangers rifle through my stuff? I want to find them, taste their blood, rip out their—

Torch? Thoughts of revenge are broken. I whisk back round and stand over a torch half hidden under a pillow. The reason why I'm here, why I came to this room, comes back to me.

'Scarlet,' yells Ethan, banging on the door. 'Let me in.'

I jerk my head around to face the noise when I catch my reflection in a fragment of broken mirror. A proud jaguar with fiery brown eyes stares back at me. My brain tries to accept the image, work out what's going on. Then before my eyes, the fur retracts, my skin bubbles. I stretch out a human arm and pluck the torch off the floor.

'Scarlet!' yells Ethan for the third time. 'You're freaking me out! Open the door!'

I clear my throat and croak, 'I'm coming.'

Unlocking the door, I find Ethan looking more pale than usual.

'What happened in there?' he says. 'I heard roars and growls and—'

'I don't know what you're talking about,' I say, trying to maintain a calm pose as I walk past him. 'I've got the torch.'

'Have you got a lion in there too?' he asks, poking his head into my room.

'Yes, I have three!'

I walk down the stairs, taking a few surreptitious deep breaths, and make my way back to the lounge.

'You are a very strange girl,' says Ethan, following me into the room.

And you don't know the half of it!

I step into the fireplace, switch on the torch and enter the six-digit code. The safe springs open and I let out a sigh of relief. Dad's laptop *is* still there. I clamber out, holding it.

'That was up your chimney?' says Ethan.

'Yeah,' I say, distractedly, not taking my eyes off the laptop. All I want to do is open it, and discover the name and hopefully the address of Dad's client. 'It was in the safe.'

'What? You have a safe up your chimney?' says Ethan.

My stomach twists. Did I honestly just tell him where our safe is?

Ethan's eyes dart between the laptop in my hands and the chimney breast. 'Why would you have a safe up there?'

'Because Dad works for a security firm. He thought burglars wouldn't think of looking up there. I guess he was right.'

'But what does he have on his laptop that is so important, he has to hide it up a chimney?'

'I don't know,' I yelp, wishing he'd stop with the questions. 'Listen, Ethan, you've helped me lots, but I'm all right now. You can go if you want.'

'I told you earlier—no way. I'm not leaving you alone in this house. I'll wait with you until your dad gets back.'

'That might be a long time,' I say. 'Seriously, I'm fine.'

Ethan folds his arms. 'I'm staying.'

By his stern expression, which actually reminds me of Dad's, I know it's pointless to argue. Plus it would be wasting precious time. 'Fine, you can stay, but I've got stuff to do. You'll have to leave me alone.'

'That's all right, there's lots of things I can do here,' says Ethan, walking towards a coffee table and turning it the right way up.

I bite my lip. I should help him, after all he is helping me, but I don't have time. I have to access Dad's computer.

'Thanks,' I mutter, avoiding eye contact as I walk past.

I make my way into the kitchen and groan. Every cupboard has been emptied, strewn across the floor. And did they really have to attack the fridge?

I flip a chair the right way up and put the laptop on the table. I lift the cover, switch it on and wait impatiently for the screen to light up. Then a word flashes up. I stare at it in horror.

PASSWORD.

How could I have forgotten? And what on earth would Dad have chosen? Clasping my head, I gaze at the screen. I'm just going to have to guess. I type in Dad's name first. 'Password incorrect. Please try again.' I try Mum's name. Nope. I try my name, my nickname. I try every freaking name and word I can think of. But nothing. Password incorrect.

'No!' I shout, slamming the table.

'Is everything OK?' says Ethan, appearing in the doorway.

'What are you doing here?' I snap. 'I told you to leave me alone.'

Ethan looks startled. 'I came to see if you had a broom. I'm only trying to help.'

'Oh . . . right,' I say, sinking into my chair. 'I'm sorry, that was awful. I'm just so frustrated. I was so close. I was . . .' My words trail away.

'Can I help?' says Ethan, softly.

I snort. 'Can you hack into computers?'

'Yeah,' he replies.

'What?' I say, sitting up straight. 'You can?'

'I've got a program back in my room.'

'You have a program for hacking into people's computers?'

'Yeah,' he says, with a smile. 'Don't tell anyone.'

'So . . . you could hack into this?' I say, tapping the laptop, my heart beginning to pound. ''Cause I can't get past Dad's password. I've tried everything I can think of, but I've no idea what word he would have chosen.'

'If he's hot on security, I imagine he would have numbers in there too.'

'Numbers? Can you still do it?'

'I guess,' says Ethan with a shrug.

'Then what are we waiting for?' I say, leaping to my feet. 'We should go to yours.'

'What about your dad? Won't he worry if you're not here when he gets back?'

'I'll write him a note,' I say.

But Ethan, he's not coming back.

CHAPTER FOURTEEN

I follow Ethan into his bedroom, and can't help grinning. Pink floral paper covers the walls. Lavender print curtains hang at the window and a matching duvet covers his bed.

'Nice bedroom!' I say.

'Oh, I begged Gran to let me have it like this,' he replies, with a smile. 'Let's have the laptop then.'

I stare at Ethan's outstretched hand and hesitate. All of Dad's data is on this computer. Do I really want someone else accessing it? I mean, how well do I know him? 'You're just going to unlock the password aren't you? You're not going to look at Dad's information?'

'Of course I'm not. And you're going to be with me the whole time. You'll see what files I'm opening.'

'Sorry, Dad,' I mutter under my breath, as I hand him the laptop.

Ethan sits at his desk. 'I need to run a program between my computer and your Dad's. This'll take some time, so you might as well sit down.'

I perch on the edge of his bed and watch him fix connecting leads between the two computers. He starts pressing buttons, loading programs, and doing other strange things that completely baffle me.

'Where did you learn to do this?' I ask.

'Mum,' he replies.

'What?' I lean forwards. 'Your mum taught you how to hack into a computer?'

'No,' says Ethan, with a laugh. He spins around to look at me. 'What kind of parent would do that? Teach their child to commit a crime?'

Oh, I wonder???

'Mum taught me how to write my own program,' he continues. 'But she doesn't know anything about this one. I designed it myself.'

'Really? I'm impressed. How does it work?'

Ethan turns back around. 'It's pretty complicated. And I could do it a lot faster if you . . . you know . . . shut up.'

I've had lots of practice keeping quiet, watching Dad. So I sit still, listening to the tapping of computer keys and the television blaring from downstairs. But now that I've nothing to occupy my mind, images of Dad seep into my brain. Is he tied up? Hurt? The delivery guy wasn't that old, but he looked strong. I bet he could inflict a lot of damage. And where is Dad? What if they've taken him abroad?

I'm going mad just sitting here. I need a distraction.

I wander over to Ethan's notice board, the only thing hanging on the wall. He's pinned so many photographs to it they're fighting for space, and I guess they're a reminder of home. They're all of Ethan surrounded by girls at a bowling alley, in a park, next to his computer. And they're all looking at him with simpering adoration. A bit like the way Amanda looked at him too.

My eyes flicker between the back of his head and the pictures. Is Ethan good looking? I suppose he is a little, I think grudgingly. If you're interested in boys, and like gelled hair and big grins.

'This is harder than I thought,' says Ethan, suddenly. 'Your dad's got some serious protection on this. And I mean serious. What's he trying to hide?' He leans his elbow over the back of the chair. 'Genuinely—what is he trying to hide?'

'Oh . . . stuff,' I say shrugging. I walk towards him and peer over his shoulder. The laptop screen is filled with numbers, letters, commands, and lots of other things I don't understand. 'Does this mean you can't do it?'

'I'm not saying that,' says Ethan, starting to type again. 'It's just more of a challenge than I thought it would be.'

His fingers fly over the keys and once again I'm torn. Part of me wants to rip Dad's files away from this computer wizard. But the other part of me needs his help. If Ethan can't get past the password, I have no idea how I'm going to find Dad.

Ethan's fingers halt, hovering above the keyboard. 'Will you stop staring? You're putting me off.'

'Oh . . . sorry,' I say, returning to his bed.

I keep quiet. Soon the tapping of keys become hypnotic, and my eyelids grow heavy. I haven't slept for ages. I fall back onto his duvet, and curl into a ball. The room feels hotter. I want to stay awake. I should stay awake. But exhaustion takes over and in minutes I'm fast asleep.

I awake with a start. Sunshine pours in through the window, and I sit up to find Ethan slumped over his desk, snoring softly. Oh God—I slept in a boy's room. Dad will kill me if he finds out! Dad! Only two days left before he needs his insulin.

I jump to my feet, when I notice the cables are no longer attached to Dad's laptop. Does this mean Ethan's done it? Padding over to his desk, I nudge the laptop awake from sleep mode. Dad's files fill the screen, and I gaze in wonder. Ethan *has* done it!

I want to wake him, say thank you. But he snores again. I should just let him sleep. I quietly lift the laptop from the desk and grab my shoes. Wearing only socks on my feet, I pad out of Ethan's bedroom, sneak down the stairs, and run straight back to my house.

Careful of the glass in the hall and smashed crockery in the kitchen, I sit at the table. I grab a packet of crisps from the floor and stuff them in my mouth. Food—finally!

Throughout his career, Dad has separated his burglaries into two categories—the unknown job, and the obvious job. The unknown jobs are the heists that no one ever knows about—not even the victims. The second category covers all the burglaries that make newspaper headlines because people notice their items have gone missing and call the police. They're the ones I keep in my scrapbook . . . My scrapbook! I'll have to check whether it's still under my bed. But right now—the laptop!

I lift the cover and once again a list of files appear on the screen: Admin, Jobs for *Safe as Houses*, Finances, Associates . . . The list is long and seemingly endless, and there's nothing entitled cat burglaries. But he wouldn't use that as a filename, would he?

I'm about to open the files randomly when my eyes zoom in on the one entitled, Jobs for *Safe as Houses*. Why would *that* be on *this* laptop? He uses another computer for work.

I take a deep breath and click on the file. House names flash up on the screen. To most people, they would mean nothing. They'd think these are the houses that Dad has done security checks on. But to me they mean more, much more. Dad and I have burgled a few. The Harlingtons' house is on there, as is the house we stole the bracelet from, plus many more properties where I was lookout. I'm guessing the other houses are the ones Dad and Mum burgled before I became his trainee.

With quivering fingers, I click on the house in Belgravia. Three names and an address appear. Along with an item. An Aztec double-headed serpent. Beginning to feel giddy, I read through the names. Lady Elizabeth Melksham, Richard Melksham, Matthew Melksham.

Matthew . . . Matthew . . . Could he shorten his name to Matt? Because that's the name the delivery guy shouted on Dartmoor. They said they had Dad.

My eyes flicker to the address. It's in the Lake District. Postcode: LA23 5ZS. To make sure I definitely have the right client, I click on the house we burgled to get the bracelet and mask. Sure enough, the same information appears. My mouth dries. Have I found the place where they're keeping Dad? Oh let him be there. At the very worst, let Matthew Melksham be there. Because then I can quiz him and find out where they *are* keeping Dad.

I grab a piece of paper and pencil and scrawl down the address, when the doorbell rings. I freeze. Is it the delivery guy coming back for me? Or Lady Melksham herself?

'Scarlet, are you in there?' calls Ethan.

My shoulders relax, and I hurry to the front door, whisking it open.

'I'm sorry I came over here without telling you. I didn't want to wake you up,' I say.

Ethan just stands there, his easy smile missing from his face.

'But you've done a great job, thank you.'

Ethan still doesn't say anything, and I realize he's looking at me with a peculiar expression on his face.

'Are you all right?' I ask.

'Your dad's a cat burglar.'

'What?' My stomach leaps into my throat.

'Your dad's a cat burglar,' he says, louder and clearer.

I peer over his shoulder. Good, no one else is in our close. I grab hold of him and pull him into the house, slamming the door behind.

'I recognize the names,' he says.

'What names?'

'The names on your dad's computer.'

'How do you know what's on his computer? You were looking at his files?'

'OK, I know I shouldn't have, but I couldn't resist. It was all so secretive. Did you know your dad has seven levels of security on his laptop? Seven different pass-words for me to hack! So I couldn't help it. I decided to have a look at what he'd worked on last. All these houses came up and when I clicked on them—'

'You clicked on them?'

'All these names came up, and I recognized them. You see—I have a game.' He waves a disc in the air.

I read the title and my breathing quickens. *Heist City*.

'It's about heists and cat burglars.'

'So? Is my dad's name on it?' I say with a sneer. *Please tell me it's not!*

'No! But it got me interested. I looked online and started Googling cat burglary, and found all these sites reporting past crimes that have never been solved. They talk about a Jing Hao painting from China, a figurine of Imhotep from Egypt, eighth-century gold earrings from—'

'So? What's that got to do with Dad?' I interrupt, trying to sound casual, but my heart is thrashing.

'Those same items are on your dad's computer, with names, addresses.'

It's like the world's exploding at my feet. Through a clenched jaw I manage to say, 'Dad isn't a cat burglar. He works for a security firm.'

'He uses that as a cover.'

My body starts heating up and I don't care that my wrist is being strangled. 'Who do you think you are? Sherlock Holmes?'

'I'm right, aren't I?' he says, stepping towards me.

I need to silence him. Blood pumps through my veins faster and faster. My body melts, bubbling like boiling wax. Fur sprouts, claws grow. I drop to all fours.

Ethan shrieks and his eyes bulge.

I lick my chops and Ethan stumbles backwards. I can hear his heart thumping. I see beads of sweat dripping down his forehead. Lifting back my head, I roar. Ethan pales. His body sways. His legs buckle and his head hits the floor.

Good—he's an easier target lying down.

CHAPTER FIFTEEN

I leap off the ground, and open my jaw ready to bite his skull. Sailing through the air, I look down at Ethan. Time seems to stand still. He's just a boy—a boy who's helping me. Somehow I manage to twist in mid-air and push myself away. I land in a heap beside him. I watch him lying on the ground, his chest rising up and down. Thank God he isn't dead. Just out cold.

I wait for a moment but when his eyes don't open I nudge him with my nose. He doesn't stir. I lick the side of his face, coating my tongue with salt. His eyes flash open. He takes one look at me and his eyeballs roll to the back of his head. He faints again.

I step backwards. Of course—Ethan needs time and space. He also needs to see a girl rather than a jaguar looming over him. I've got to turn back, but how? My

102

mind sweeps over each time I've transformed and I realize there's a possible solution.

Spinning around, I bound into the lounge, over to a large fragment of mirror. I stare at my reflection. A wildcat stares back. Come on—where's the real me? At last the fur recedes and my skin becomes smooth. The hair on my head grows longer, my claws disappear, and I stand up on two legs.

'Scarlet,' croaks a voice.

I turn around to see Ethan leaning against the doorframe, his face deathly pale.

'What just happened?' he asks.

I open my mouth but the words stick in the back of my throat. What exactly am I going to say?

'Am I going mad?' he asks.

It would be easy for me to say yes, tell him he was hallucinating, but then I think of how he's helped me with Dad's computer. Instead I shake my head. 'You're not going mad. I might be, though.'

Ethan swallows. 'Did you . . . did you turn into a . . . a leopard? You were standing in front of me and then—'

'I wasn't a leopard.'

'Oh God, I am going mad,' he says, slamming his head against the door frame, closing his eyes.

'Ethan, I didn't change into a leopard. I was a jaguar.'

His eyes fly open and silence echoes around the room.

'Wow!' he says, finally.

'It's a bit crazy, isn't it?'

'Oh—only a little bit,' he says, throwing me a weak smile. 'Jaguars can break skulls with their teeth, you know.'

'No, I didn't know that,' I say, refusing eye contact. It was his skull that I was instinctively going for.

'Have you always been able to . . . change into a jaguar?' he says,

I shake my head. 'This is very new to me, too.'

'How can you? Why do you?'

I can't answer the first question, not to him anyway, but the second is relatively easy. 'It happens when I need something. Or want something.' Thinking back to when I tried to move the log burner, I add, 'Although it doesn't always work.'

'What did you need or want from me?'

'You don't want to know!'

'Don't I?' He rubs the back of his head and winces.

'Are you hurt?' I ask, taking a step towards him.

Ethan jumps backwards, his hand shooting out in front of him. 'I'm fine. You stay where you are.'

'I'm not going to hurt you,' I say, but I stop moving. 'I just wanted to check your head, to see if it's bleeding. You hit it hard.'

Ethan reaches behind his hair again. 'It's not wet. There's no blood.'

'I think you should sit down. You look really pale.'

'I wonder why!' says Ethan, with a snort.

He turns around. At first I think he's going home—I won't blame him if he does—but instead he staggers into the kitchen. I follow him, making sure I keep my distance. He collapses into a chair and I lean against the counter. Then both of us glance at the laptop on the table. He nudges it, waking it up. From my position, I can't see what's on the screen, but I know what Ethan is looking at—the name and address of our client who wanted the Aztec artefacts.

'Is your dad OK?' says Ethan. 'Is he here? Or is he still at the police station?'

'He's not at the police station.'

'No, I guess he can't be, can he?' Ethan laughs, a slightly hysterical bark.

'What?'

'Oh the irony. The cat burglar's house is burgled.'

I feel blood pump around my body, and I take a deep breath. I can't afford to get angry.

'Your dad is a cat burglar?' says Ethan. 'I'm right, aren't I?'

I press my lips together. Is there any point in lying?

'I'm not going to tell anyone. I just want to know the truth,' he adds.

Trying not to think about what Dad would do to me, I give a small nod.

'Wow!' says Ethan again, slapping his hands together. 'So your dad is a cat burglar and you're a cat.'

'I'm a human!'

Ethan raises his eyebrows. 'Half human, half cat,' he concedes.

I fold my arms. 'Ethan, you're taking this all very well, especially my—' I search for the right word, '*transformation*. I would have thought you'd be running from the house screaming by now.'

Ethan's face breaks into a grin. 'Why? This is the most exciting thing that's ever happened to me.'

'I'm glad you're enjoying it!' I snap.

'Plus, I have a game.'

'I know. *Heist City*.'

'No, another game. The life of a shape shifter. Me and my friends used to play it back home in Cheshire. I'd become a tiger or a wolf.'

I stare at him without blinking. 'So . . . because you have a game, you're not surprised that I can change?'

Ethan shrugs. 'I was surprised at first, but now it feels kind of natural.'

'Natural?' I explode. 'You really live through your computer!'

Ethan's grin stretches even bigger. 'Not any more. From now on, I'm going to live through you.'

And suddenly we both burst out laughing. The tension drains away and I can almost taste the relief.

'So what now?' says Ethan, his eyes flicking back to the laptop.

'Are you going to go to the police?'

'No,' he says, sounding hurt that I've even suggested the idea.

'Then I've got to find Dad.'

'Don't you don't know where he is?' says Ethan. 'Can't you just ring him? Try him on his mobile?'

'He doesn't have a mobile,' I say. 'I don't, for that matter.'

'What?' Ethan's jaw drops, and if possible, he looks more shocked now than he did when I transformed into a jaguar.

'You're not going to faint are you?' I say.

'How can you not have a mobile?'

'Because we don't want to be traced. And, Ethan, if Dad did have a mobile, do you think the kidnappers would let him answer it?'

The incredulous look on his face drops to one of sheer horror. 'Your dad's been kidnapped? I thought he was away . . . preparing for a heist or something. Oh God, Scarlet!'

The images of Dad being tied up return. 'Dad's been taken,' I whisper, falling into the seat opposite Ethan. 'I have to get him back. That's why I needed you to help me get into his computer. The last job he did went very wrong. His clients weren't happy and . . . and they've taken him.'

Ethan swallows. 'How did it go wrong?'

I drop my head into my hands and peer through my fingers. 'He . . . he lost the Aztec artefact.'

'How can he lose an artefact?'

He didn't. It was me. Pangs of guilt return. 'It's a long story, and right now I don't have time to tell you about it.'

'But you definitely know he's been kidnapped?'

I nod.

'And you don't want to go to the police?'

'I can't! If they manage to save him, they'll lock him up straight after.' I thump the table with my fist. 'I've got to do it. I've got to find him and bring him back.'

'Oh no,' says Ethan, shaking his head violently, 'you can't! You're just a girl.'

'No I'm not. I'm also half cat, remember?'

'Scarlet, I'm not joking. How old are you?'

'Thirteen.'

'A year younger than me. You can't rescue your dad.'

'I'm not joking either. I have to do it.'

'You need help.'

'From who?' I say, lifting my hands into the air. 'There's absolutely no one I can ask.'

'Well . . . what about me?' says Ethan.

'You?' I stare at him in surprise. How could he possibly think some computer geek like him could help someone like me?

'Do you know how to operate your dad's surveying equipment?' he asks.

'His what?' I say, sharply.

'Your dad has some amazing software on his computer—he can upload plans of houses.'

'How the hell do you know that?'

'Last night before I fell asleep, I went though your dad's computer.'

'You did what?' I explode. 'I thought you only looked at what he'd been working on last!'

'Just hear me out,' says Ethan, lifting his hand flat against the air to silence me. 'I found a programme that lets your dad access the planning office. I could upload the plans of the house where your dad's being kept.'

That's if he is there! I slam the worrying doubt to the back of my mind. 'Can't you do that for me now if I tell you the address?' I say.

'I could but it'll take a long time to run. I could do it on the way to the house.' He looks back at the computer screen. 'You said it was an Aztec item. Are these the people—Lady Elizabeth Melksham, Richard—'

'Yes,' I say cutting him off before he runs through the entire family.

'They live in the Lake District. How are we going to get there?'

We? I glare at him. 'You know this is real life? This isn't like one of your computer games. If something goes wrong, it really goes wrong. You can't start again.'

'Of course I know it's real!'

I close my eyes. This is, without a doubt, a reckless move. But . . . if Ethan can get the plans of the house, I won't be going in blind.

'All right, you can come,' I say.

'Oh yeah!' he yells, punching the air with his fist.

My stomach clenches. Have I just made a stupid mistake? 'There is one condition,' I tell him, quickly. 'You have to do everything I say. No arguing. No deviating.'

'I can do that,' says Ethan.

'We might be gone a few days. Will your gran mind?'

'I'll go and ask her. I'll tell her that you and your dad have invited me to go somewhere. It shouldn't be a problem.'

'What about the party tonight?'

'As if I care about that now!' he says. 'So what's the plan?'

I look at the clock—the only thing still hanging on the kitchen wall. Obviously the burglars didn't think we'd have a safe hidden there. 'Listen, we don't have much time. I need to get to Dad as soon as I can. I'll meet you outside your house in half an hour. Pack a bag with everything you need. If you have any surveillance equipment or programming or whatever stuff goes with Dad's laptop, bring it along.'

'Will do,' says Ethan, leaping up. He glances at his watch. 'I'll meet you outside my house in twenty-seven minutes. Zero nine hundred hours!'

'This isn't a game!' I snap, as he waltzes out of the room.

CHAPTER SIXTEEN

Now that I'm going to do something, I feel energized. Rushing back into the lounge, I grab my rucksack. I already have the grappling hooks but now I shove in the torch I used earlier. Returning to my bedroom, I snatch my balaclava and black clothes off the floor. Scrabbling about the carpet, I search for a screwdriver, pliers, picklock, and knife. Who knows what I'll need? It's better to be prepared. I peer under my bed and see my scrapbook still in its place. Part of me wants to bring it. Part of me knows I should destroy it. In the end I leave it exactly where it is.

Then I go into Dad's room. My heart stops. The burglars weren't content with emptying cupboards and shelves. They slashed his bed and chair apart. Feathers from pillows and his duvet cover the floor.

I hurry over to Dad's bedside table. It's upside down; the drawers and contents sprawled across the floor. Kneeling in front of it, my throat tightens. Please still be here. I turn the bedside table the right way up and feel the inside of the base. Using my nails, I locate the square rim. The bedside table has a fake bottom, with a small wooden box fitted inside. I dig it out and lift the lid. Thank God—there are the keys. But there's no money. Normally Dad keeps at least three thousand pounds in here.

Oh well. At least I have transport.

There are still twenty minutes to spare so I jump in the shower. Once dried, I put on normal jeans—not a nine-hundred-pound pair—and a plain T-shirt to blend into the background. I race out of the front door, and then twist around. How could I have forgotten?

Hurtling back into the kitchen, I look at the counter top. My stomach crumbles. The insulin box isn't there. OK—that means it's been knocked onto the floor. Oh God—that means the glass bottles are probably broken.

I shove food packets, broken plates, knives, and forks to one side. Then I spot a white box under the table. Hardly daring to breathe, I yank it open. To my utter relief, the medicine bottles are still in their compartments, totally intact. *Finally luck seems to be on my side.* I stuff the box into my bag and rush back outside to our neighbour's drive.

Dad pays Mr Nagimuru rent for the car space. It's our second car, a Ford Fiesta. Not too modern. Not too old. No one bothers looking at it.

I scribble a short message onto a scrap of paper and shove it through the letterbox, telling Mr Nagimuru I'm taking the car for a few days. I sign it from Dad. Mr Nagimuru has no idea what Dad and I really do, and I don't want him finding out now.

When I press the button on the key fob, the locks spring open. I jump into the driver's seat before someone can spot me. Putting my bag and Dad's laptop onto the backseat, I reach for the road map we keep tucked under the passenger side. After a few minutes, I locate the Lake District and work out a rough route, very rough. Hopefully, Ethan is good with maps. I turn on the engine.

I pull out of the drive with a few kangaroo hops and park next to number four. I look at my watch. 9.03. Ethan is late. Dad wouldn't approve.

Finally I see him hop over the hedge. His toes hit a bramble and he trips, sprawling onto the ground. His bag flies through the air. *Seriously?* He's clumsy. He's late. Why am I letting him tag along?

Ethan clambers back to his feet, grabs his belongings, and makes his way to the pavement. He looks towards my house but ignores the car and me. I want to beep but that would attract attention. I switch on the engine again and crawl next to him, winding down the window.

'What are you waiting for?' I ask.

Ethan jumps back. 'You're driving!' he splutters.

'Yep. Well, I would be if you hurried up and got in.'

He scrambles around to the passenger side and dives in. Before he's closed the door, I put my foot on the accelerator and speed off, this time without kanga-roo hops.

'When did you . . . ? How did you . . . ? You're only thirteen! Can you even see over the dashboard?'

'I can now. I used to have to sit on a cushion when Dad first taught me.'

'When was that?'

'When I was eleven.'

'Wow!'

A small part of me smiles. Ethan is staring at me in awe. It's a strange but nice feeling having someone impressed with what I can do. All the time I was training when I was ten, eleven, twelve—Jules and Charlie had no idea.

'You are one crazy girl,' says Ethan. 'Do you even know where we're going?'

'We've got to get to the Lake District. So that's two motorways and—*No way!*' We haven't even left the vil-lage and there's a police car parked on the side of the road.

'Don't worry. He's not looking for you,' says Ethan. 'He'll be looking for a wildcat. It's been all over the news. A wildcat was seen on a train and—'

He stops, and we both glance at each other. I can't help smiling.

'OK, he probably *is* looking for you,' says Ethan, his eyes beginning to sparkle. 'But he thinks you're a wildcat. Just stay calm and don't panic.'

I look straight ahead, and thankfully the policeman ignores us.

'There might be journalists and police all around here now, so don't speed,' says Ethan. 'Make sure we're not pulled over, 'cause you really don't look old enough to drive.'

'I do know that,' I say.

We pass reporters with cameras and more police, but luckily no one looks in our direction.

'Why were you a cat on the train?' asks Ethan.

'I was dodging the fare.'

'Seriously?' He catches my eye and we both burst out laughing. 'I bet that's a first for the railway company!' he says, at last, shaking his head.

When suddenly I smell something awful. 'Something stinks!' I say. 'It's like . . . vinegar and chemicals.'

'Oh!' says Ethan, his hand flying to his head. 'That might be my hair.'

'Your what?' I glance left. Ethan's hair is now all spiky. 'Is that why you were late? You were doing your *hair*?'

'I was getting ready.'

I snort loudly. 'Well I'm glad you're so prepared. As long as your hair's all right, we have nothing to worry about!'

CHAPTER SEVENTEEN

The first part of the journey runs smoothly, much to my amazement. We leave the police and reporters far behind, and I get used to the smell of hair gel. Ethan appears to be busy, tapping away on the laptop, so maybe he isn't going to be a complete waste of space.

'Do you have any money?' I ask, as we reach the first motorway.

'I've brought as much as I had in my room. Seventeen pounds and fifty two pence.'

'Oh!' My stomach clenches. I had hoped he'd have more.

'That's not a problem, is it? You must have money.'

'Why?'

'Because your dad's a thief,' he says easily. Too easily. I grit my teeth. 'He's not a thief. He's a cat burglar.'

'What's the difference?'

'Are you kidding? The difference is—he doesn't destroy property. He doesn't destroy people's belongings.' I think of Mum's photo lying on the floor, and a sour taste fills my mouth. 'Dad works out what he wants, where it is, and often the crime goes undetected.'

Ethan's brow furrows. 'How can someone not notice their things are missing?'

'Because Dad gets replicas, and puts them back in the same place.'

'He's still stealing though, isn't he? He's going through their stuff. I saw your face when you realized the burglars had been in your bedroom. You looked sick. And you growled.'

My gut twists. As much I hate to admit it, Ethan has a point. But I say, 'You don't know what you're talking about. You don't know why Dad's a cat burglar.'

'Why is he then? Why does he steal?'

'He doesn't steal! He's on a mission. He returns arte-facts back to their rightful owners.'

'What?'

'He returns artefacts that were stolen—taken by invad-ers, or during wars, or even by modern-day thieves. He returns them to their rightful owners—to family members who've been searching for them. That Jing Hao painting you saw on Dad's laptop—that was stolen twenty years ago by some businessman in New York. Dad was contacted by the descendent of Jing Hao and employed to get it back. I'd say the descendent had the better claim, wouldn't you?'

I glance at Ethan and his eyes are wide open.

'Why don't people just go to the police?' he says. 'Try to get their stuff back legally?'

'They've often tried. That descendent of Jing Hao tried. But the businessman had paperwork showing ownership. It's just the paperwork was fake.'

'And you know that for sure?'

'Yes! Well . . . Dad does. He does so many checks on people before he'll take on a case. He wants to make sure that he's working for the right side.'

'But what if he gets it wrong?'

'He doesn't!' I say, flatly.

Ethan shakes his head in disbelief, then exhales loudly. 'Wow! The world you live in!'

'Well you're not exactly perfect. You hack into computers.'

'Yeah, but I don't do anything once I'm in. I never alter or steal anything.'

'So you just do it for fun? For a game? That figures!'

I grasp the steering wheel even tighter. My knuckles whiten. Are Dad and I just common thieves?

We fall into silence. Ethan starts typing again and I slam my foot down on the accelerator.

Ethan leans over and peers at the dashboard. 'You're speeding. I thought you were. You've overtaking everyone.'

I bite my tongue. Is he going to knock everything I do?

'Hey, you weren't the getaway driver, were you?' he asks.

My heart stops. His words are mocking and I know he doesn't believe it. But that was my first job after Mum—

'In all seriousness,' says Ethan. 'Slow down! We don't want to get caught on a speed camera or pulled over by the police.'

I scowl. He's right of course. I take my foot off the accelerator and move the car back into the slow lane. Silence ricochets around the car . . . again.

'This is strange,' says Ethan, suddenly. He's frowning at the laptop. 'The programme's loaded and I'm looking in the planning office, but there's no record of a house being at that address in the Lake District. The area is completely empty. It's just hillside.'

'It can't be. Have you tried LA23 5ZS?' That postcode is imprinted on my brain.

'Yeah. I used the full address your dad has in his records. I've checked it five times.'

'There must be a house there. Why would Dad put a fake address into his private file?' But as I say these words, ice flows through me.

'You know, you seem to be speeding up again,' says Ethan.

I look at the speedometer and wrench my foot off the accelerator. Without realizing, I was driving over one hundred miles an hour.

'Hey, what's that orange light for?' says Ethan.

'What orange li—' I look down and my heart flies into my mouth. 'Oh no! We're running out of petrol. We must have at least five cans in the garage back home.

Why didn't I pick some up?'

'That's all right. We can buy some more.'

'With what? Seventeen pounds and forty-two pence?'

'Seventeen pounds and fifty-two pence,' corrects Ethan.

'How are we going to get to the Lake District on that?' I say.

Then I notice a service station looming upon us. I yank the steering wheel, pulling us into the slip road.

'What are you doing? You can't steal petrol,' says Ethan, as I drive into the service station.

'I know that,' I say. 'Are you hungry?'

'Always.'

'Right then, I'm going to drop you off here.' I stop the car at the far end of the car park, away from prying eyes. 'You can get us some burgers and chips, veggie for me, please. And I'll pick you up at this very spot in twenty minutes.'

'You're not going to steal petrol are you?' says Ethan. 'That's illegal.'

'So is driving at the age of thirteen. But you don't seem to mind.'

CHAPTER EIGHTEEN

Ethan climbs out of the car and I pull away. At the edge of the services, we passed a hotel where cars can stay overnight. If I leave Dad's car there, it won't attract attention.

Outside the hotel I scan for cameras. Good—there aren't any. I slot Dad's Fiesta into a space amongst a group of other cars, before grabbing our rucksacks and laptop. Ethan's bag feels light and for a moment I wonder what he's brought with him.

Walking amid the other cars, I search for one that won't stand out. Halfway down, between two people carriers, I spot it. An old silver Ford Focus. Both colour and make are incredibly common. Plus it isn't alarmed. I only hope the owners are staying at the hotel for at least one more night, and won't miss it until tomorrow.

I'm not used to doing this in daylight but I don't have much choice. I look around. No one's nearby. With my fist, I bang the side of the door hard and the lock pops up.

I scramble into the front seat. Thank God I brought pliers. Bending down, I reach under the steering wheel and rip off the black casing surrounding the steering column. Three pairs of coloured wires dangle down. Oh God! Which colours do I need? Closing my eyes, I think back to training. Got it! I grab the two cables and cut them with the pliers. OK – here goes. I take a deep breath and touch the two wires together. There's a flash. I squeal in delight. I can't help it. I touch the wires together again and this time the engine springs to life.

I sit up straight, put the gearstick into the reverse position, and then pause. I may have done the hard part, hot-wiring the car, but now I have to escape without being seen. For all I know, the owners are looking out of their hotel window. Checking again to make sure the coast is clear; I slowly slide out of the parking spot. To my relief, no one shouts, no one runs towards me. I drive through the service station, almost bouncing in my seat. If only Dad could see me now.

I head to the spot at the far end of the car park. Ethan's already there, holding a brown bag of food. But I don't believe it. He's surrounded by girls. They're all looking at him adoringly, listening to every word he's saying.

My jaw clenches as I park five metres away. I wait for him to run towards the car, but instead he carries on talk-ing to the girls. Whatever he says makes them laugh. My jaw clenches even tighter. What if I just left him? Then I think of the housing plans on Dad's laptop. I couldn't find them without his help. I hate to admit it, but I need him. And so I roll down the window a few centimetres.

'Ethan,' I call.

He scans the area for a moment but takes no notice of the car.

I roll the window down a little further. 'Ethan, hurry up!'

This time he looks at me. He looks at the car. His eyes widen. And to my horror he shakes his head.

'Ethan, we don't have time for this,' I shout. 'Get in!'

The girls turn to look at me now. Their eyes also widen. 'Who's that? Is she old enough to drive?' they ask.

I glare at Ethan.

He clears his throat and says, 'That's my older sister. She looks young for her age.' Before the girls can say anything else, he scoots around the back of the car and leaps inside, dropping the brown paper bag into the foot-well.

A mixture of chips and hair gel hits my nose. Ethan's obviously found the time to fix his hair before getting food. I slam my foot on the accelerator. The wheels squeal on the tarmac and people from all over the service station turn to look. Oops! I lift my foot off the pedal and drive more smoothly.

'You stole a car!' he exclaims.

'And you almost got me caught. I can't believe you were talking to those girls. Have you ever heard of a secret mission? You know, the type of mission where we don't try to grab attention? Where we don't worry about what our *hair* looks like?'

'Well you obviously don't,' he says.

'You're right—I don't. I just want to find Dad,' I say, as the car hits the motorway.

'So you stole a car?'

'You told me I couldn't steal petrol!'

'Very funny!' snaps Ethan. He throws his head back against the seat. 'I can't believe I'm in a stolen car.'

'You're the one who wanted to come. I wasn't going to bring you. Now I wish I hadn't.'

'But now I'm an accomplice to a crime.'

'Yep, you're implicated.'

Both of us sit in silent rage.

'What about the owners of this car?' says Ethan, suddenly. 'What if they need it to get home? What if they have young kids? Now they're stranded.'

'They don't have kids. They don't have any car seats or crumbs on the backseat.'

'But what if they need to get somewhere desperately and now they can't?'

My throat tightens. I hadn't thought about the impact on the owners at all.

'They're probably staying at the hotel,' I say. 'And once I've found Dad, we'll make it up to them. We'll get a present. We always do. Dad will be able to trace them.'

'Yeah, I bet he can!'

'Ethan, I didn't have a choice. I have to find my dad,' I say.

Ethan lets out a huge breath. 'I know you do. But a car! I wish you'd stolen petrol now.'

'There were cameras in the forecourt, but there weren't any in the hotel car park.'

'You sound like a professional. How do you know how to steal a car anyway? Did your Dad teach you?'

My muscles tense and I don't say anything.

'He did, didn't he?' Ethan's jaw drops. 'You're his partner, aren't you? I can't believe it's taken me this long to figure it out.'

'I'm not his partner,' I whisper.

'Yes, you are!'

My body heats up. My breathing quickens. Oh no—I can't transform while I'm driving. I look in the rear-view mirror and stare at my reflection. The heat fades.

'So?' says Ethan. 'Are you going to tell me the truth?'

I need to change the subject. I remember his bag on the backseat. 'What have you brought anyway? Your bag's really light. Let me guess, you've brought your computer games and some pyjamas.'

Now it's Ethan's turn to be silent.

'You have, haven't you? Did you bring anything else? Like a knife or even a screwdriver?'

'Hey, I'm not the thief here. What have *you* brought, anyway?'

I can't take my hands off the steering wheel to stop him. Ethan pulls my bag off the back seat and opens it. His eyes bulge. I know he's seen the grappling hooks, the NVGs, the screwdriver.

'You really are a pro,' he says, breathlessly. 'What have you got me into?'

'I haven't got you into anything. What did you think this was going to be like? You saw the state of my house. You know my dad's been kidnapped.'

Ethan starts gulping for air.

'I mean, how can you—' I stop talking. Ethan's face is turning blue. 'All right, all right,' I say in a softer voice. 'You need to calm down. You need to take deep breaths.'

I jerk the steering wheel and pull us onto the hard shoulder.

'My inhaler!' he gasps.

Snatching his bag, I rummage inside. I whip out his inhaler and he grabs it.

'You're asthmatic?' I say.

Ethan nods as he takes a few puffs. I watch him, anxiously, waiting for his breathing to slow down. At last it's under control.

I lay my head on the steering wheel. 'At least you brought something useful with you.'

'Hey, I also brought my toothbrush.'

I look at Ethan out of the corner of my eye. Seriously— why did I let him tag along?

CHAPTER NINETEEN

'Are you OK?' I ask. We've been sitting on the hard shoulder for about five minutes. 'You look better.'

'I guess. I mean I can breathe now,' says Ethan. 'And I'm getting my head around you being a master criminal.'

I bite my tongue.

'It's just I've been thinking. Can you steal any car?'

'Pretty much. Some have alarms and you have to disable them. But Dad and I don't bother with those.'

'But could you disable an alarm and take *any* car?'

'Yes . . . why? Do you want to learn how?'

'No!' exclaims Ethan. 'It's just if you could steal any car, why did you steal this one? You could have stolen a Ferrari or . . . or an Aston Martin. I saw one of those back at the services. We could be travelling in style.'

'Yes—because that wouldn't be noticeable! Ethan, you do realize we're trying to blend into the background, not stand out?' I tilt my head. 'So let me get this straight. You are completely against thieving of any kind, unless it happens to be hot-wiring a sports car?'

Ethan grins. 'I guess my ethics disappear if I can go in an Aston Martin.'

'At least you're honest,' I say, with a laugh. 'And if you're feeling better, I don't suppose you'll pass me some food.'

'Oh I forgot about that. I never forget about food.' He opens the bag and delicious smells of burgers and fries drift out.

'Sorry it's cold,' he says, handing me my burger, when suddenly he sits up straighter, and looks around. 'Aren't you going to move the car? The hard shoulder isn't a safe place to stay on.'

I burst out laughing. 'Ethan, I'm a cat burglar. Do you honestly think the hard shoulder worries me?'

His face reddens and he doesn't say anything else.

Still chuckling, I bite into my burger. I expect to relish the taste like I always do, but it tastes so bland. Something smells far more appetizing. I glance at Ethan's burger oozing with meat juices. I want to rip it out of his hands and—

Stop! I tell myself. *I'm a vegetarian.*

I try to force my taste buds to enjoy the rest of the veggie-burger, but fail miserably. And so I start the car, feeling completely unsatisfied. In no time at all we reach the second motorway.

'Scarlet, I've got to ask you something,' says Ethan. 'Is there anything else you haven't told me about yourself? Because if there is, tell me now. I don't think I can cope if you spring it on me.'

I peer at him out of the corner of my eyes. He already knows so much, is there any harm in saying more? 'I can change into an eagle.'

Ethan exhales loudly.

'And I may be able to transform into other creatures too.'

'You may?'

'Yeah, but who knows when and where!' All at once the words tumble out. I tell him everything. By the time I've finished, my jaw aches, but I feel slightly better. I glance at Ethan. Does he believe me? 'What are you thinking?' I ask.

'I'm thinking I should make a computer game of your life.'

'Hah!' I snort.

'Really—I'm thinking I should get back on your dad's laptop and see if there's something else in the planning office, something I've missed.'

'Sounds good,' I say, stretching out my back. Then I groan. My body aches from all this driving, which isn't exactly ideal before a rescue.

'Are you all right?' he asks.

'I'm a bit stiff, that's all.'

Ethan looks out of the window. 'No way! We're nearly in Cheshire.'

'So?' I say, squirming in my seat.

'That's where I live, but my parents are away. Why don't we stop there for a bit? You could rest, or even have a sleep, and I could work on your dad's laptop. Then we could go to the Lake District at night—'

'Under the cover of darkness. That still gives me a day to get Dad his insulin. Ethan, that's brilliant!'

Ethan looks surprised. It occurs to me that this is probably the first time I've ever said something nice to him. Maybe I should try a bit harder.

'You have to take the next exit,' he says, a grin stretching across his face.

Ethan's house is a smart detached red brick in the middle of a leafy street. I park the car on the road, a little distance away. Grabbing our bags, we climb over his gate.

'You, hide under there,' I say, pointing to a large rhododendron bush at the edge of his front garden.

Ethan frowns, but darts under the bush while I stalk around the back of the house. The windows are locked—I hadn't expected anything else—and I would never smash a downstairs window. I crane my neck, glimpsing the edge of a skylight. All I have to do is get up on the roof and break the glass. I creep back around the house and under the bush.

'Which room is the skylight in?' I whisper.

'Mine,' says Ethan.

'Oh! Sorry about that.'

'Why?'

Without answering, I say, 'You stay here as lookout, I'll scale up to the roof and—'

'Can you do that?'

'I'll open your window. I think I'll have to smash it, but we'll board it up afterwards in case it rains. Normal burglars won't try to get in through there.' I pause. 'So? What do you think?'

Ethan wrinkles his nose. 'Well . . . it sounds like a great plan, but wouldn't it be easier to use these?' He brings his hand out of his pocket and dangles a set of keys.

'You have a key? Why didn't you say so?'

'This is my home—of course I have a key. You never gave me the chance. You sent me over to this bush.'

'Oh!'

'So instead of you scaling the roof and smashing my window, why don't I just use the front door?'

He clambers out from under the bush and with a smug swagger makes his way to the front of the house. I follow behind, well aware my face is flushed, wanting nothing more than to rugby tackle him to the ground.

CHAPTER TWENTY

Ethan's house looks like it belongs in a magazine. Every-thing is minimal, white, and showroomy. Expensive furniture. Expensive accessories. As we walk through the white hall, I pop my head into the lounge to see white sofas, clear glass coffee tables, and an enormous television on the wall.

'Your gran must love that,' I say.

'She does. She never leaves this room when she comes to stay.'

Ethan leads me up the stairs, and suddenly there's colour. On the landing walls are three brightly coloured paintings.

I peer at them closely. 'These look expensive.'

'Yeah,' says Ethan, casually. Then his face falls. 'I mean—no, they're not. They're nothing special. They're not worth stealing.'

I turn to him in horror. 'Do you honestly think I would steal from you? Did you not hear me when I told you Dad and I only return stuff back to their rightful owners?'

At least he has the decency to look sheepish. 'Sorry,' he mutters. 'You're in here,' he adds quickly, opening a door.

I'm instantly hit with clutter. The room is crammed with furniture, make-up, books, guitars, CDs.

'This is my sister's,' explains Ethan. 'She's away at university but has a toddler fit if anyone changes her room. Mum can't stand it.'

'I didn't know you had a sister.'

'No, I don't like to talk about her.' He leans against the door frame. 'Dad thinks she's so perfect. He never saw her smoking or picking on me when she lived at home. You're an only child, aren't you?'

I nod.

'Lucky,' he says.

'Does your mum think she's perfect too?'

'Not so much. She sees through her.' He pauses. 'What's your mum like? You haven't really mentioned her.'

'So where are you sleeping?'

He looks at me and I know he's going to ask about Mum again. I glower at him and fortunately he gets the message.

'In my room at the other end of the hall,' he says, finally. 'I'll leave you to it. You could do with some sleep. You look knackered.'

'Thanks!'

I enter his sister's room, and dodge the musical instruments and piles of books, before collapsing onto her bed. It sways and gurgles beneath me. Whoa—she has a waterbed. Now that I'm lying down, I desperately want to sleep. But as soon as I close my eyes, an image of Dad tied up fills my brain. I roll over, water sloshing in my ears. Yet all I can see is Dad's stricken face. I toss and turn. As much as I want to, I don't think I'll ever get to sleep. But slowly the ripples grow soporific. My thoughts of Dad become distant. And a dream consumes me.

I'm standing in front of an altar, in a stone chamber—a pyramid. A pot of bubbling golden liquid hangs over a fire pit before me. On the other side of the flames are four men dressed in long black robes. Mosaic masks cover their faces. Each mask has a different turquoise animal stone in the centre.

'It is time,' I say, although the words come out in a strange language.

We lift our right arms and the stone flints in our hands glint in the firelight. We hold out our left arms above the pot, and I nod. We slash our arms with such force, blood pours out. The pain sears. But as I watch the red hiss and spit with the bubbling gold, the anguish is worth it.

I seize a wooden staff off the stone altar, and with two hands stir the liquid. The blood and gold fuse together.

I bend down and inhale the steam. From one breath, I feel the power of man, of animals, of gods running through me. Releasing the stick, I stretch out my arms. Claws rip through my fingers. *Wait until the bracelet is fully formed*, I think. *Wait until we've added our animal stones. What will happen to me then?*

'Scarlet.'

I hear a name being called in the distance. I close my eyes, angry at the intrusion. The voice grows louder, insistent. Yet so am I. I'm not ready to leave this chamber.

'Go away!' I yell, swiping the air with my claws, but the words don't come out as I expect.

An angry roar reverberates from the back of my throat, jolting me awake. I sit up in bed to find Ethan two metres away, looking terrified. His arm is outstretched, shaking uncontrollably. A mug lies on the floor with deep scratches across it, and steaming brown liquid has been sprayed across the room.

'I . . . I brought you a cup of tea,' he stammers.

I slam my hands to my mouth. 'Oh Ethan, I didn't hurt you, did I?'

'No. Only the mug, though I think you were aiming for me.'

'I'm sorry. It's just I was having a dream. I was in this Aztec temple and there were—'

I stop. I can hear a hissing sound coming from beneath me. My eyes flicker to the bed. Without realizing, I've clenched my fists and grabbed hold of the mattress. My claws ripped through it and now bubbles of water are trickling out.

'I've destroyed your sister's bed,' I yelp in horror.

If possible, Ethan's face pales even more. 'Right, I think we'd better leave this room. I'm going to deny we ever came here.'

'Do you want me to smash a window? We could pretend burglars did it?'

'Why would burglars scratch her bed? I've got a better idea. I'm going to blame the next door neighbour's cat.'

I carefully climb off the bed, making sure I don't touch anything else, even though my nails have reduced to normal size. Then I notice the darkening sky through the window. Glancing at my watch I see it's half past nine. Have I been asleep all that time?

Then I remember. 'How did you get on with Dad's laptop?' I ask.

Ethan grins. It must be good news.

I follow him into the lounge and sit on the sofa opposite the coffee table. Dad's laptop rests on top of it.

'While you were sleeping,' he says, 'I decided to use Google Earth to see if I could find the house. I don't know why I didn't think of it earlier.'

'Google Earth?'

Ethan shakes his head. 'What century do you live in? Google Earth is an internet site where you can zoom in on locations via satellite. You can look at pretty much any address in the world.'

'Isn't that snooping?'

'Legal snooping. Anyway, I put Lady Melksham's address in, and straight away I found the house.'

Instantly I'm paying more attention.

'I found a mansion in massive grounds—with a huge wall around the outside—at least four times your height. Then I noticed this little icon on your dad's screen and I pressed it. This is what I found.' Ethan nudges Dad's laptop awake and a 3D image of a room fills the screen. 'Lady Melksham's study.'

'No way! Google Earth can take inside pictures! That can't be legal.'

'No! Google Earth can't do it. Your dad did it—seven years ago. He has these intricate computer generated images of all the rooms, of all the security, of every CCTV camera. He knows this house inside and out.'

'But why? How?'

Ethan shrugs.

I lean forward. Ethan taps keys and various rooms—a kitchen, a lounge, a bedroom—come into view.

'I don't understand. Why would Dad have done this?'

Again Ethan shrugs. 'Do you think he might have burgled them before?'

'I don't know. Normally he doesn't burgle his own clients.'

'Well, whatever the reason, this really helps us,' says Ethan.

We scrutinize Dad's plans. It's a three-storey stately home, with turrets, Georgian windows, and loads of chimneys. It's split into the east wing and the west wing, with massive staircases running in between. As well as the usual rooms like bedrooms, bathrooms, a kitchen and a dining room, there's a library, a ballroom, art gallery, and wine cellar.

'Where do you think they're keeping Dad?' I ask.

'In the ballroom,' says Ethan, at once. 'Or the cellar.'

'Why?'

'According to your dad's plans, the ballroom is sound-proofed, so if he screamed, no one would hear.'

My stomach heaves and the revulsion must show on my face.

'Not that your dad would be screaming,' he adds, quickly. 'I mean why would he scream? No, I'm sure—'

'Why the cellar?' I interrupt.

'Because he'd be underground and no one would see him.'

I shudder.

'Sorry.' Ethan frowns and looks away.

I clear my throat and say, 'So which room should I try first?'

'In all honesty, I would try the ballroom.'

I wrap my arms around my body and nod.

We look at the plans for half an hour more, and I try to memorize the layout of the rooms. 'It's time to go,' I say at last.

But as I stand, I can't take my eyes off the laptop. Why does Dad have these images on his computer?

He wouldn't have burgled his own client. Would he?

CHAPTER TWENTY-ONE

Two hours later, we're driving through the Lake District. I'm dressed in black, with a map and torch balanced on my legs. It turns out Ethan isn't that great at map reading. After we got lost for the second time, following his directions, I decided to take over.

Ethan sits beside me, still glued to Dad's laptop. He's trying to learn all he can about the house.

'Found out anything useful?' I ask.

'Who's B.W.?'

My body tenses. 'What files are you looking at? You're only supposed to be looking at the house.'

'Your dad transfers thousands of pounds to B.W.,' says Ethan. 'Who is it?'

'What is it! Not who is it!'

'OK—what is it?'

I hesitate. 'If you must know, B.W. stands for Born Wild. It's a charity helping the welfare of wild animals. Dad donates a tenth of all the money he makes to it.'

'Really?' says Ethan. 'Why?'

'Because . . . because Mum used to work for them before she died.'

'She died? Oh Scarlet, I'm so sorry. I didn't know.'

'Why would you?' I snap. Then in a softer voice I say, 'She died three years ago in a car crash.' And suddenly, in my mind I see her. We're baking chocolate chip cookies at night. We're wearing NVGs.

'Are you OK?' asks Ethan.

'I miss her. We used to do so much together.' A lump forms in the back of my throat. 'Dad and I didn't really have that much to do with each other. And after she died, he had *no* idea what to do with me. We didn't talk. We moped around.' I clear my throat. 'But then there was this one day—I was climbing trees in the woods behind our house, and I didn't know he was there. But he'd been watching me. He said I was a natural, and showed me his grappling hooks. From then on, he taught me how to hot-wire cars, use glass cutters. It was something we could do together. It took our minds off Mum, while still keeping her close. If that makes any sense?'

'Yeah, it does, actually.'

I snigger. 'Some dads teach their daughters to play chess. Dad taught me to burgle.'

'So . . . you're telling me cat burglary is a hobby?' says Ethan, and I can hear the grin in his voice.

'Yep, a hobby!' I reply with a laugh.

'How old were you?'

'Ten.'

'Whoa!'

'I didn't go on an actual heist with him then. I only started that last year.'

'Only when you were twelve then!'

'Before we decided to move, Dad gave me the choice. Did I want to be a normal girl having friends, going to school without secrets or did I want to become his accomplice? I chose the second.' I pause. 'Mum was his accomplice before the accident.'

Ethan is silent for a while and I guess he's taking it all in.

'I wish I had something in common with my dad,' he says at last. 'I don't think I'm the kind of son he thought he'd have. He thought I'd be playing football or rugby, or even better—boxing.'

'Boxing?' I exclaim.

'Can you imagine? With my weedy arms?' says Ethan, with a sad, bitter laugh.

I regret my response instantly. 'Ethan, I bet he is proud of you. You just don't know it. I mean—you're fantastic with computers. What kind of parent wouldn't love that?'

'He doesn't.'

I glance at him. Even though we're driving through the dark, his face is lit up in the laptop screen. He looks utterly miserable. Is Dad proud of me? I wonder.

'Maybe you should tell him about your hacking,' I say. 'That would impress him.'

Ethan snorts and when I look at him again, he seems to be . . . smiling?

'What's so funny?' I ask.

'Nothing,' says Ethan, his smile vanishing.

'You do get on with your mum, though, don't you?' I say, trying to cheer him up. 'She gave you those games and she must love computers.'

'Yeah, Mum and I get on all right,' he says. 'She gives me games that most parents wouldn't. Like the—' He stops talking. Instead he stares at the screen. 'Scarlet, did you say that your dad donates a *tenth* of everything he earns?'

'Yeah.'

'He donates a fortune! Each time he sends thousands—and that's just ten per cent of his income. *How* much does he earn?'

'I've no idea. Dad always deals with the money side.'

'I can see he only steals to help rightful owners get their stuff back! There's nothing in it for him!' he says, his words dripping with sarcasm.

'I never said helping rightful owners wasn't profitable!' I snap, no longer feeling sorry for Ethan.

But as we drive in silence, something inside of me squirms. Just how much does Dad charge for the jobs? Is it for the equipment or our safe houses? Or is there a part of him that does it to get rich? No, it can't be. He only does it to help rightful owners. We're carrying out a service. We *are* helping people.

'I don't think you should be looking at those files,' I say, angrily. 'Do you have any idea what Dad would do to you, or to me for that matter, if he knew you were on there?'

'Point taken,' says Ethan, and he quickly presses a button.

I lean across and see Lady Melksham's ballroom filling the screen.

'Keep it like that, we're nearly there.'

The road grows steeper, windier, narrower. We really are heading into the middle of nowhere. Then we turn a bend and gasp.

CHAPTER
TWENTY-TWO

Illuminated in the headlights is a giant stone wall, at least six metres high, with state of the art security cameras towering on top. There's no sign of the house. It's fully hidden.

I switch off the engine, cutting the headlights, not wanting to be caught on video.

As if reading my mind, Ethan says, 'We're all right here. The cameras only pivot 180 degrees. They can only zoom in on the house, garden, and interior wall.'

'How do you know that?' I ask.

'It's on your dad's laptop. He's marked down all the security—the cameras dotted along the perimeter wall; the doors and windows that are alarmed.'

'Ethan, why are you only telling me this now?'

'I didn't think it was important.'

I stare at him. 'How could you think those details were not important?'

'Because they're not going to disrupt your plans.'

'My plans?'

'You do have plans, don't you? Aren't you going to turn into an eagle and fly over the wall? Or morph into a jaguar, eat the kidnappers, and rescue your dad?'

'I haven't really thought about it,' I say. 'It sounds like you have, though. You want me to eat someone?'

'What do you mean you haven't thought about it?' says Ethan.

'I haven't had time. I was too concerned with getting here. But if you're quiet for a minute, I'm sure a plan will come to me.'

I gaze at the wall, the enormity of what I'm about to do hitting me hard.

'You said you were an eagle, right?' says Ethan.

'I knew you couldn't be quiet!'

Ignoring me, Ethan says, 'Why don't you change into a bird and fly in through the chimney?'

'I don't think it works like that. I can't change on demand. I have to *really* want something, like when I changed into a jaguar and wanted to rip out your skull.'

Ethan's hands fly to his head. 'I didn't know that's what you wanted to do.'

'Sorry,' I say, not feeling sorry at all.

'But don't you really want something now? Don't you really want to rescue your dad?'

His words slam into me. And of course he's right. I open my door.

'What are you doing?' says Ethan.

'I'm going to try to transform.'

I walk to the front of the car and stand with my back to it. Ethan shines a torch in my direction. I glance up at the security cameras, grateful they face only one way. Taking a deep breath. I stretch out my arms, and start to flap like I have a pair of wings. Closing my eyes, I whisper, 'I want to fly, I need to fly.'

Nothing. No heat. No strangling. But to be honest, I'm not really surprised.

My arms fall to my sides and I trudge back to the car, dropping into the driver's seat.

'I'm going to have to climb over the wall,' I say.

'What? You can't,' yelps Ethan. 'Not in human form. The cameras will catch you climbing down the wall or running across the garden.' He switches on the indoor light. 'Now don't get mad, Scarlet, but I've had a thought. What if your dad isn't even in there? What if he's been taken to some other place?'

'I've already thought of that,' I say, 'but that *is* Dad's client's house. So even if Dad's been taken, they'll know where he is.'

'But what if they're not there?'

'Then I'll search the house for clues. But Ethan, I don't know how and I don't know why, but for some strange reason I know Dad is in there. Call it gut instinct. Which is why I'm going to have to go over the wall. I have to get to Dad before tomorrow, before Friday.'

Ethan frowns. 'It's Friday today.'

'No it's not. It's Thursday.'

Ethan shakes his head. 'It's Friday,' he says, opening the laptop, pointing to the date.

Every single droplet of blood drains from my body. It *is* Friday. But I woke in the field on Wednesday. No—I didn't. I fell from the sky on Wednesday, but woke in the field on Thursday. I can't breathe. I clutch my stomach.

In the distance I hear someone saying, 'Calm down. Do you need my inhaler?' A hand rubs my back. 'Calm down,' I hear again. 'We can work this out.'

I try to breath slower.

'I can help you. I think there's a way in.'

I instantly focus. My breathing normalizes. 'What did you just say?'

'I think there's a way in,' says Ethan. 'I think there's a way in,' says Ethan. 'I wasn't going to tell you because it's so risky, and I thought you were going to be an animal. But if my calculations are correct, there's a blind spot in between two cameras about a hundred and fifty metres from here. I've looked at their trajectories and the views from the cameras don't quite meet.'

'Are you serious?'

Ethan nods. 'If you climb over the wall at a certain spot, and run in a straight line, you can get to the house without being seen.'

'Oh Ethan, I'm so glad you're such a geek!'

'Cheers!' he says, looking rather put out.

147

'So where's this spot?'

'Opposite these trees,' he says, turning the laptop in my direction.

Two large trees with thick twisting branches fill the screen. One of them leans on a wooden support, unable to stand on its own. They're pretty recognizable.

'OK, let's do this,' I say. 'I need to get to Dad now.'

I reach for my rucksack. Ethan does the same.

'Err, I reckon you can leave that here, unless you're planning on having a sleepover,' I say.

'Very funny,' says Ethan, but he drops his bag.

We climb out of the car and I put on my NVGs.

'You need to switch off the torch now or you'll give us away,' I say.

'But I can't see a thing.'

'Hold my hand. I'll guide you.'

'Oh? So you want to hold my hand?' says Ethan, a smile creeping into his voice.

'Now I want to rip it off!' I snap, switching on my NVGs.

I think about leaving him here, but I could do with a second opinion about the trees. So I grab hold of his hand and pull. He trips over a tree root.

'Watch where you're going!' I snap.

'I can't,' he retorts.

At first we don't walk that fast since Ethan keeps stumbling. I know it's not his fault, but I'm greatly relieved when his eyes become accustomed to the darkness. Speeding up, we make our way around the edge of the big wall, looking out for the trees.

And then I spot a tree leaning on a support. I look to Ethan for reassurance.

'That's them all right,' he whispers.

'OK Ethan, I'm going in now. Go back to the car and wait for me there. And . . . thanks for everything.'

I turn to face the wall, look up at the peak, and gulp. This is it—I'm going to find Dad.

CHAPTER TWENTY-THREE

I aim the grappling hook and press the button. The hook whizzes out of the end and clamps round the flat stones at the top of the wall. Adrenalin coursing through me, I raise my legs and storm up the side. At the top, I crouch down, waiting for the sirens to wail. Silence swoops around me. Thank God Ethan found the precise blind spot.

Stuffing the hooks back into my rucksack, I stare at the house. It's further away than I thought, but even from here, the size is overwhelming. Then my stomach clenches. There are countless chimneys on the roof. Which one do I need? What if I go down a flue that leads to a bedroom, and wake someone up? I'm ridiculously unprepared. Dad would have done more research.

I'm going to have to wing it.

Grabbing the second grappling hook, I set the timer on the handle to one minute and the distance of the wire to five metres. Hooking the clawed end onto the edge of the wall, I throw the handle over the side. It plunges down, stopping a metre above the ground.

I abseil down the wire, and jump to the lawn. The grappling hook releases, shoots back into the handle, and drops to the grass. I shove it into my bag, and then make a run for it.

That's when I hear barking. I turn to see six Dobermans charging towards me from the side of the house. What are they doing here? Dad didn't mark out any kennels . . . or warnings.

I don't have long to think. All I know is that I can't keep running forward or I'll meet the dogs head-on, and I can't deviate from the straight line or I'll be caught on camera. There's only one option left. I spin around and hurtle back towards the wall. My feet pound the grass. My arms slice through the air. I plead for my legs to run faster, but the Dobermans are closing in. Their snarls rip through me.

Suddenly, claws hit my back. For a split second, I fear I'm going to be trampled, devoured. But in that instant, my temperature rises and pain sears around my wrist. My body liquefies and I twist out from under the weight of the dog.

I stretch out a pair of long brown wings and soar into the air, higher and higher up the side of the wall. The

Dobermans howl beneath me. I feel so powerful, so free. Shooting through the sky, I can see for miles through the darkness.

'Scarlet, are you all right? I can hear barking,' shouts Ethan.

My head jerks round, and my eyes zoom in on Ethan facing the wall, his hands flat against the stones. I remember why I'm here.

'It's all right, I'm fine,' I yell, swooping towards him, but the words come out in a high-pitched squawk.

Ethan dives to the ground.

'It's me!' I cry, but he can't understand.

I don't have time to try again. This might be my only chance to get into the house undetected. I swirl around and fly back over the wall, over the yowling dogs.

Bolting straight for the roof, my eyes flicker from one chimney to another. One flue sticks out larger than the others. With any luck it'll lead to the dining room or a lounge. Tucking my wings in, I shoot through the chimney. My body spins as I hurtle through the soot. I feel a whoosh of fresh air as I near the fireplace. Spreading out my wings, I soar into the room. It's a bedroom rather than a dining room, but thankfully it's empty.

I fly over to the window, and look out, trying to gain my bearings. I figure I'm on the middle floor, but is it the east or west wing? The ballroom is on the ground floor, so I should just search for some stairs.

Soaring over to the door, I stop. Eagles and doorknobs do not go well together. I'll have to transform back into a girl. Scouring the room, I spot the small mirror on the dressing table. Perching on the stool, I look into the glass and see a magnificent eagle with powerful wings and deadly talons.

Staring into the eyes, my body grows hot. My feathers liquefy and soon I'm a girl wearing NVGs and a rucksack. I jump off the stool and creep across the carpet. I feel more vulnerable now. I can't see as well. I can't hear as well. Plus, as a human, I can easily be caught.

Pausing outside the door, I listen for sounds on the other side. Nothing. Hopefully, everyone's asleep. I turn the doorknob and push it open. The hall is empty, but as I look left and right, I still have no idea which way to go. Deciding on left, I take a few steps, when I smell it. I double over and grasp my stomach. It's as if someone's punched me. This is the smell of death. Oh God—please let Dad be OK.

I race down the landing, following the stench. It grows stronger, viler. Saliva wells up in the back of my throat but I force myself to carry on. Bursting through a door, I slam my hand to my mouth. The smell is unbearable . . . but I can't see anything dead. I walk past a bed with rumpled covers. On the wall above the bedhead, instead of a picture, is a long brown gun. Strange choice of artwork.

The smell seems to be coming from another door on the opposite wall. Trying not to gag, I whisk it open. For a moment my heart leaps—Dad isn't in there! But my relief is short-lived. I'm looking into a walk-in wardrobe. Fur coats line the rails. Tigers, leopards, mink . . .

I stare at them in horror. My body grows hot and the strangulation of my wrist begins. I want to find their owner, tear out her—

No! I slam the door. I can't do this. I have to find Dad. I stagger backwards, staring into a mirror on the wall, before rushing out into the hallway. Once again I'm completely lost, but now my brain feels fuzzy. I can't even remember which way I came from. Images of dead tigers, leopards, and mink fly through my brain. I have to get away. I run down the corridor, past door after door, and out of sheer luck arrive at a giant staircase.

The stench of death fades and my brain begins to function. I think back to the plans on Dad's laptop. The stairs swoop above me and below me, running through the centre of the house. Now I know exactly how to get to the ballroom.

I creep down the staircase into the entrance hall on the ground floor. There are giant windows covered with thick velvet curtains, and a closed door leading to the front garden, leading to safety. Instead I choose the door to my right, the door that should lead to the long narrow library. But the room's completely empty. It doesn't even have furniture, carpet, or curtains, let alone books.

I tiptoe inside. There are deep scratches in the wooden floor; so deep I see them through my NVGs. Have the Dobermans been in here?

I hurry across the room to the door that leads to the ballroom . . . and hopefully to Dad. My breathing quickens. I grab the handle and turn, but I don't believe it—the door's locked. I rummage through my bag, searching for the pick, when I hear footsteps on the staircase. I search more frantically but the footsteps are getting closer. I spot the pick but it's too late. I won't be able to undo the lock in time. Looping around, I stare wildly. There's nowhere to hide. Maybe the person will go the other way. But their footsteps grow closer.

Then to my relief, I feel the telltale signs. My temperature rises. My wrist hurts. This time I don't try to fight it. If I'm found in this room, I'd rather be an eagle or a jaguar. I can fly or attack my way free.

Almost instantly I'm on all fours and closer to the ground, my sight unaltered by the darkness. I lift my head, suddenly aware of strong, powerful smells. Wee, salt, blood. *What?*

Then the door opens. I crouch low to the floor. A tall, muscular guy steps into the room. He smells of hair gel, aftershave. Not death. But I know who he is—the delivery guy.

He switches on a light and I blink, momentarily dazzled. He steps forward and then stops, his eyes widening. But for some strange reason he doesn't look scared or shocked. Just a little . . . surprised?

I lean back on my haunches, ready to pounce.

'How the hell did you get out?' he says.

His words stop me in my tracks. What does he mean?

He lifts his arm. He's holding a long black pole with two prongs sticking out of the end. He presses a button and blue light zips between the prongs, and I hear the sizzle of electricity sparking. He has a Taser, a stun gun.

A growl rips from the back of my throat.

His face pales and he swallows. I think he's going to turn around, make a run for it. But to my astonishment, he shuffles forward, thrusting the Taser at me.

'You know what this is? You know what it can do?' he warns.

I growl louder.

The electricity flickers closer to my face, and I step backwards.

'I'll do it. I'll stun you,' he says, 'unless you go back in there.' He waves the Taser in the direction of the ballroom.

I turn my head to the locked door. Well . . . I want to go in there, anyway. And so I allow the delivery guy to herd me across the room. He pulls a key out of his pocket, opens the door, and I pad inside. The light's already on and the room feels heated.

Five steps in, I forget about the Taser, the delivery guy. Instead I stare around the room. Smells assault my nose; noises deafen my ears. My brain can't compute what it's seeing.

But I do know one thing—this isn't a ballroom.

CHAPTER TWENTY-FOUR

Large cages line the walls, with a walkway running in between.

'Come on,' says the delivery guy.

I sense the Taser inches from my fur, and step further into the room. On my right there are three enclosures. Two large wildcats with tawny coats and black rosettes pace up and down the first. So that's why the delivery guy wasn't surprised to see me. He thinks I'm one of them.

Next to the jaguars in the middle cage are six monkeys. They have furry white faces and shoulders, and black bodies, tails, and tops of heads. They're capuchins—I know because I helped Mum look after one.

From where I am, I can't see what's in the third cage. So I turn my head left. *Am I dreaming . . . ?* This isn't a cage with bars, but a glass aquarium. Two alligators thrash their tails in shallow water.

'I said, come on,' says the delivery guy, pressing the Taser again, dangerously close to my fur.

I pad along the central aisle, unable to take my eyes off the reptiles, when I hear a squawk from a far enclosure.

The delivery guy speaks again but for the first time his voice is tender. 'Itzca, I'll come see you soon.'

There's another squawk, louder, indignant.

'I'm sorry,' says the delivery guy with a chuckle, 'I miss you too. But I have to deal with this first.'

He eyes me warily, and then glances up at the side of the aquarium. His face falls. 'I don't believe this. The keys aren't there!' He curses. 'I left them in my other jeans.'

I turn to see an empty hook halfway up the side of the aquarium.

Waving the Taser at me, he says, 'You're going to have to wait here till—' Then he stops. His jaw drops. He's looking past me, into the cage behind. He curses again. 'We get another jaguar and no one bothers telling me!'

With the Taser still pointing at me, he walks backwards, towards the door we came through. He pushes the door and it remains open. I make to follow him, when there's another outraged squawk. I hesitate. I want to know what the remaining creatures are. I have a pretty good idea, but I have to make sure.

Bounding down the aisle, I look into the third cage on my right. Two golden eagles perch on fake branches, their eyes haunting and unblinking. One of them starts squawking. I'm guessing it's Itzca. Then I hear a howl.

Twisting around, I see four wolves standing directly behind the bars of a cage, their yellow eyes appraising me. The largest wolf howls again.

My chest tightens. *I'm sorry I can't rescue you. I've come for Dad.*

Then there's a creak. The door's closing. Tearing down the aisle, I manage to slip into the empty room just in time. Thankfully the delivery guy's facing the other way. He throws open the door to the entrance hall and disappears into the other half of the house. I bolt straight for the curtains opposite the stairs.

Hidden in the velvet, my mind goes crazy. Why are all these animals here? They must have something to do with the bracelet, but for the life of me I don't know what. I snap my teeth. I shouldn't be worrying about them. I've come here for Dad.

Creeping forward, I stick my head out beyond the curtains and sniff the air. But there's no way I'll be able to smell Dad from here. The animals stink too much. So I flick back my ears, focusing on sounds instead. A quiet moan comes from upstairs. I'm not sure it belongs to Dad, but it's a start.

Bounding up one flight of stairs, the moaning grows louder. I run down the landing, past closed doors, and catch a whiff of Dad's cologne. My pulse races. So Ethan and I were wrong. Dad isn't in the soundproof room or the cellar.

I stop outside a door, where Dad's smell is so intense.

I inhale deeply. He's alone—I think. Then I growl inaudibly. I want to kill whoever invented door handles. Because now I need to be human again.

Swooping around, I look into the window. The dark night is behind it, but my reflection in the glass is clear as day. A proud, noble jaguar stares back at me.

Come on, transform!

My ears draw back. My hair grows. My night-vision goggles reappear. And as a human I open the door.

My heart stops.

Sitting with his back to me, on an upright wooden chair, is a man. His feet are bound together with thick chains. His wrists are handcuffed behind his back and a black scarf is tied around his mouth. His head is slumped.

'Dad,' I murmur.

I run to the front of the chair. My throat constricts. My body numbs. It's like I've been slammed with the delivery guy's Taser.

Dad's eyes are closed and his head droops sideways onto his shoulder. His cheeks are bruised and blood dribbles out from under the gag. How *dare* they?

Dad's eyes shoot open. For a moment they're filled with sheer poison, but then the look turns to wonder.

'Dad,' I whisper.

Leaning over him, I untie the knot behind his head. The scarf floats to the floor. Without it, his face looks even worse.

'Scar,' he croaks.

'Are you OK?'

'How did you get here?' he rasps.

'Through the chimney. Listen, we don't have much time. I don't know when they'll be back,' I say, diving into my bag.

Thankfully this time I find the lock pick in seconds. I go to the back of his chair and shove the pick into the handcuffs. Locating the gears, the handcuffs fall apart. Even I'm surprised by my speed.

Dad shakes out his arms and rubs his biceps. 'What are you doing here?'

He seems stunned, not thinking. This isn't the Dad I know.

'You need your insulin,' I say, pulling out the medicine box. I hand it to him but the white box slips through his fingers onto his lap.

'You need your insulin,' I repeat, picking it up.

'You do it,' he whispers.

I freeze. I've watched Dad prepare his insulin hundreds of times, but he's never injected in front of me. *Now he wants me to do it.* I look at him searchingly. His eyes are glazed. Is it his diabetes? I know I'm a few hours late but surely he can't be too affected by it. No—it must be the Melkshams! What have they done to him?

Dropping to my knees, I open the box and join the two pieces of kit together.

'I'll . . . I'll inject your stomach,' I say, my heartbeat racing.

Dad nods and pulls up his shirt. I gasp at the bruises. 'You can do this,' he whispers.

With trembling fingers, I shake the contraption. Before I can change my mind, I plunge the needle into his skin. The insulin disappears into his body. I pull out the needle and return the device to the box.

'Good girl,' whispers Dad.

It actually wasn't as bad as I thought it would be. But now I have to get him out of here.

Dad's legs are at a funny angle, bound together with a thick chain, tied to a front leg of the chair. I shove the pick into the padlock, searching for a cog, a lever, something to turn. Nothing happens.

'Do you want to try? You're quicker than me,' I say.

He takes the pick from me but his fingers fumble even more than mine. Normally he could do this sort of thing in his sleep.

I take the pick back and try the lock again, scrabbling frantically. Sweat drips down my back. My eyes well up. I have to get Dad out now.

Then I hear footsteps on the landing. Someone's coming. I yank the NVGs off my head—if they switch on the light, I'll be blinded. They snag my balaclava and it comes off with them. My hands automatically fly to my face, trying to hide.

Someone steps into the doorway and flicks on a light.

CHAPTER
TWENTY-FIVE

Lady Melksham stands in the entrance to the room. Well . . . I'm assuming it's her. She's tall, incredibly slim, and about Dad's age. Even though it's the middle of the night, her hair is styled into a perfect brown bob, and her face is plastered with blue eye shadow, mascara, and glittering red lipstick. She wears a pale blue silk trouser suit with navy stilettos. Her eyebrows are raised and her mouth is open.

'Why aren't you going in?' asks someone out on the landing.

I watch the woman's face transform as she tries to compose herself.

'It appears we have a visitor,' she says in clipped tones, as if she belongs on a 1930s film set.

My breathing shallows.

A boy peers over her shoulder. Messy black hair. It's Matt—the boy who tried to catch me on Dartmoor. Now he has a black eye.

'You!' he shouts, sliding past the woman. 'You did this!' He points to his black eye, glowering at me.

'I thought you ran into a tree,' says the woman.

'I—' The boy stops and looks at the floor.

'So a girl did this to you?' She tilts her head and not a single hair moves out of place. Her eyes bore into mine. 'I take it you are Scarlet McCall?'

There doesn't seem to be any point in lying, so I nod.

The woman smiles coldly. 'Well, I never expected this. I was about to send my boys off again to find you, to bring you here. You've saved me the trouble.'

'What do you want with her?' says Dad. 'It's me you need.'

'Yes, but you are not being very helpful.' She walks towards us, her heels making small indentations in the carpet.

Even though I'm kneeling at Dad's feet, she isn't looking at me. Her eyes are focused solely on Dad's face. This might be my only chance. I slip the pick back into the padlock and to my astonishment the hook connects with a cog. Finally! I twist it a little, and the cog begins to turn.

The woman clears her throat. 'We thought that if you had something to lose, like your dearest darling daughter, you might become a little—ooh, how should I put it—*cooperative*.'

164

'Melksham, don't you dare use her!' yells Dad. *So it is Lady Melksham.*

Dad bolts upright, wrestling in his chair. The chains keep him in place but the pick falls out of the padlock. Nooooo!

'Where's the scarf?' demands Lady Melksham suddenly. 'And where are your handcuffs?'

She takes another look at me before her pointed shoe connects with my waist. I tumble backwards, dropping the pick.

'Don't!' cries Dad, wrestling even harder. 'If you touch her again, I'll kill you.'

'Are you honestly threatening me?' sneers Lady Melksham. She lifts her arm and to my horror I see she's holding a Taser. She slams it into Dad's shoulder. There's a sickening sizzle and Dad's body jerks. His top half collapses over his knees, like a ragdoll. I can see him breathing, but his eyes are closed.

My fear vanishes. Instead I feel pure anger. My body begins to burn, my wrist aches and my nails grow . . . but I can't do this now. I can't let them see me transform. My secret will be out. I'm not willing to kill to silence them. I need my reflection. Twisting around, I see a mirror on an empty dressing table and stare intently into my own eyes. A rush of relief cascades over me as my nails recede. Only then do I turn back around.

'Oh Matthew, I'm sorry. I was going to let you shoot him this time,' says Lady Melksham, putting the Taser on the dressing table.

Matt flinches.

'He's never used it on a human before,' she explains.

Then her eyes drop to something metal glinting on the floor. I spot it at the same time. I scoot forward on my knees, stretching out my arm. She takes two giant strides and her foot stamps on the object. My heart pounds. She bends down and lifts up her shoe. Within seconds, her fingers clasp the pick and she's standing up again.

'What do we have here?' she asks, opening her palm. 'Oh my!'

'What is it?' says Matt.

'A professional picklock.' She looks at me, her eyes piercing. 'Is this yours or your father's?'

I don't say anything.

'It's yours!' A wicked smile tugs on her lips. '*You* are his partner. I've been asking him for days who his partner is since his wife died, but he wouldn't say.'

I stiffen. How does she know anything about us?

Lady Melksham shakes her head in disbelief. 'How ingenious to have a twelve-year-old girl for a partner. You're small—you can get through tiny gaps. No one would ever think you're involved.'

'I'm thirteen,' I say.

'Well, doesn't that make all the difference!' She puts the picklock on the dressing table and gazes at the window. 'How did you get in here anyway? All my doors and windows are alarmed. Plus we've got the dogs. We've had them ever since we were—' her eyes flicker to Dad, 'burgled. How did you get past them?'

I put on a blank expression.

'Were you the one who set them off? Why didn't they maul you to death?' she asks.

I show no change of emotion and her lips purse.

'I told you she was quick!' says Matt. 'She must have outrun them, like she did with us on Dartmoor.' He looks pleased. I wonder how much of a hard time she gave 'her boys' when they came back empty handed.

Lady Melksham smirks. 'She didn't just outrun you, though, did she? She punched you.'

Matt flinches again.

'You're quite the little cat burglar, aren't you, Scarlet? Escaping dogs. Getting into my house without setting off alarms. Maybe I should employ just you next time. Not bother with your dad.'

Next time? Does this mean she's not planning on killing us?

'But I guess that depends on your cooperation,' she says, folding her arms. 'Do you know why I have your father here?'

Even though I have a pretty good idea, I shrug.

'Look at his wrists,' she says.

Edging closer to Dad, I lift up one of his arms. It's a dead weight. He's still unconscious.

'How long will he be like this?' I ask.

'Not long,' she says, dismissively. 'The voltage wasn't that high.'

'It was high enough!' I turn his wrist over and my stomach heaves. There are scratches all over them, as if someone's been trying to dig something out. 'Was…was that the handcuffs?' I ask, trying to sound innocent.

'No. We were looking for something,' says Lady Melksham.

They know the bracelet sinks into skin. The blood drains away from my face and I drop my head, trying to hide behind my hair.

She leans over; her face so close to mine her breath tickles my neck. 'You know what I was digging for, don't you?'

'No!'

She grabs a handful of my hair and pulls it back, thrusting my face upwards. 'Yes, you do. Did you see your father put the bracelet on? Did you see it absorb into his bloodstream?'

'No! I didn't!' I say, and this time I'm telling the truth.

'I don't like liars,' she says, shoving my head forward, letting it go. 'But I do like strong girls, willing to take risks, willing to lose everything. You remind me of me.'

I'm nothing like you.

'I like your father too—we go back a bit—which is why I haven't cut off his hand to get the bracelet. Yet that will be my next move if he doesn't give it up. A one-handed cat burglar won't get very far.'

Cold fingers grip my heart.

'Come with me. I want to show you something.' She looks back at Matt before adding, 'If McCall wakes up, stun him. We'll be back soon.'

Matt's face pales as if the thought sickens him. That's a good sign. Hopefully he'll leave Dad alone.

Lady Melksham takes my hand and pulls me to my feet. Even through my leather gloves, her grasp feels icy. She leads me out of the room, and guides me down the corridor until we reach the far end of the house. I'm sure this is where the art gallery is. Two ornate wooden doors block our path.

'I had these imported from Mexico. They were on a church, but they look much better here, don't you think?'

'What doors do the church have now?'

'I have no idea and don't really care.'

She places an outstretched palm on each door and pushes. The doors whisk open and she strides through them. I follow quickly before they fly back into my face.

I stare in astonishment. This isn't an art gallery. It's an Aztec museum. Large woven tapestries hang on the walls; enormous stone sculptures of jaguars, monkeys, warriors line the perimeter. In the centre of the room are rows upon rows of tall glass cabinets with aisles in between. Jewellery, weapons, and small statuettes fill the shelves. But it's the smell that's overpowering. It's like I've walked into a burning pine-forest.

'What *is* that smell?' I ask.

'Copal,' says Lady Melksham, pointing to a small pot resting on a plinth at the back of the room. 'Incense the Aztecs used.'

Even though there's only a whisper of smoke, I feel like I'm drowning in it.

'What is this place?' I ask, with a cough, looking around.

'This is my shrine to the Aztecs.' She throws me a sickly sweet smile. 'Like the Aztecs, I will sacrifice anything to get what I want.'

A cold chill runs down my spine.

'Aren't you supposed to be sending this stuff to Mexico?' I say. 'Isn't there some descendent of a high priest waiting for them?'

'Your father thinks so, but there's only me.' She strides into the centre of the room. 'When I knew what I wanted, I sent out feelers, trying to gauge who I should employ. One name kept popping up as being the best. McCall. But I also heard how he only ever stole items back for their rightful owners. So I concocted a little story about a priest. Your father lapped it up.'

'But Dad does thorough checks on his clients.'

'Not thorough enough,' she says with a laugh.

My fists clench. 'Did he get all of this for you?'

'Oh no. I also know some other thieves, although your father *was* the most professional.'

There seems to be a roaring in my ears. I want to rush towards Lady Melksham, punch her, when all thoughts disappear.

For there, lying on a glass shelf, are four terrifying masks made from turquoise, onyx, and real animal teeth. I shuffle dazedly towards the middle mask. The jaguar mask. I can't take my eyes off the hole in the centre of its forehead, and my dream comes back to me. The priest, Achcauhtli, must have taken out the animal stone and put it in the bracelet.

'You recognize this!' says Lady Melksham.

'Dad stole it for you.'

'Yes, he stole two items that day. This jaguar mask and something else. I didn't get the *something else.*'

Her words hang in the air.

'Do you remember what the other item was?' she asks, finally.

I turn to look at her, a lie forming in the back of my throat, when I gasp. A brown pouch with yellow powder lies on a shelf directly behind her. 'That . . . that bag was in the British Museum.'

'Yes, I have the real thing. They have the fake,' she says lazily. Then her eyes harden. 'What were you doing in the British Museum?'

My insides squirm. That was a foolish mistake. 'I . . . I was trying to find Dad. I was following all the trails I could. I knew you were after Aztec artefacts so it made sense to go there.'

'Clever,' she says. But her eyes harden even more. 'Did you talk to anyone there?'

'No!'

'Did you look up any information? Read about the legend of the bracelet? The bracelet you and your father are keeping from me.'

'We don't have it,' I say.

'Oh really? Your father telephones me the night of the heist to let me know you have it. And the next day it disappears. Do you think I'm stupid enough to believe he lost it?'

'That's what happened,' I yelp.

'What happened is your father put it on! Should I go back to him now? Cut off his arm?'

I need to change the subject fast. My eyes dart around the room and fall on the shelf of masks. 'There's another mask like those four . . . in the museum. A wolf mask, made from onyx.'

'A wolf mask?' Lady Melksham's eyes begin to gleam manically. 'A wolf mask? Are you sure? Are you telling me that the last mask is here? In England?'

Without bothering to hide my disgust, I say, 'You're going to steal it, aren't you?'

Lady Melksham's eyes gleam even more. 'Oh, *I* won't. I'll get someone else to do it for me. Like your father, for instance.'

CHAPTER TWENTY-SIX

'Dad wouldn't steal from a museum!'

'Wouldn't he?' says Lady Melksham, with a laugh. She points to the brown pouch. 'Guess who stole that for me? I'll give you a clue. You're related.'

'You're lying!' I say, but dread squeezes my heart.

'I'm really not.'

All at once, Lady Melksham pinches my cheek. I feel like I'm stuck in the grasp of a viper.

'Oh you look so disappointed,' she says. 'I wouldn't be if I were you, though. I imagine you've profited well from me. Saying that, my boys were a little surprised when they saw your house. They thought you'd be living in a castle for what your father charges me.'

I jerk my head out of her grip. 'Why do you want the bracelet so much anyway?'

'Isn't it obvious?' she says. 'I want to make the Aztecs the supreme race once more. I want to be like the god Tezcatlipoca—ruling the fates of mortals.' Her voice becomes higher, hysterical. 'I'll transform into animals, scare humans into doing what I want.'

I step back from her—just how mad is she? When all at once I remember I shouldn't know any of this. 'What . . . what are you talking about? How can you transform into an animal?'

'Because the bracelet has powers! Magical powers.'

I look at her as if she's crazy, which isn't that hard to do, when a thought hits me. 'But if a bracelet's sunk into someone's skin, how can they get rid of it?'

'They have to truly want to. They have to visualize it leaving their bloodstream.'

Really? Is that all I have to do?

'Of course that will only work if they haven't transformed yet. Once they have, the bracelet is stuck with them for life.'

For life?

I gulp for air. Fog clouds my brain.

'But there's no chance your father could have transformed yet. He hasn't got the masks.'

'What?'

'All five masks unleash the powers of the bracelet. And the fifth one is at the museum!'

What the heck is she talking about?

Lady Melksham tilts her head. 'You know—you look as if you don't believe a word I'm saying. I'm going to ask you one last time. Did your father put the brace-let on?'

'No!'

'Hmm, I need to see him *now*.' She grabs me by the hand and drags me out of the room into the corridor.

My body instantly feels stronger. My lungs clear of incense. I hadn't realized how weak I was feeling until now. But my brain is going crazy. According to Lady Melksham, I need all five masks to transform. But I don't have one, and I change the whole freaking time!

She pushes me into the room, where Dad is awake, sitting up. I silently thank Matt for not stunning him. Dad's hands are fastened behind his back again, but the scarf remains on the floor. My head clears and I rush to his side. His skin looks paler and the bruises stand out even more.

'How are you feeling?' I ask, dropping to my knees. 'You were electrocuted.'

'I'm fine . . . really fine. What about you?' His eyes fall upon my cheek. 'Your scar. Did she do that?'

For a moment I don't know what he's talking about. Then I remember falling out of the sky. I trace the hard skin across my cheek and say, 'No, don't worry about it.'

'Oh isn't this touching?' says Lady Melksham, wandering over to us. 'Such love between a father and daughter. Such protectiveness of a father . . . who takes his daughter out with him on heists. Matt, I told you to stun him if he wakes.'

'I—I—' stammers the boy.

'Oh, don't look so worried. I'm actually pleased you didn't,' says Lady Melksham, 'because then I couldn't do this.'

She steps closer to Dad, the Taser back in her hands. She'd better not use it on him again. Her hand lifts, but instead of aiming at Dad, she aims it at my head. My wrist tightens.

'What are you doing?' yells Dad, wrestling with the chains and handcuffs.

'I don't want to use it on her,' says Lady Melksham, 'but I will.'

My body heats up.

'McCall—purify your blood,' cries Lady Melksham. 'Give the bracelet to me. It's what you want to do.'

She's testing him!

I need to stop my transformation. The mirror is directly behind Lady Melksham, so I shuffle left, kneel up straight, and look at myself.

'Do it, Dad. Show her you don't have it,' I say.

From my position, I can also see Dad's face in the mirror. He closes his eyes, holds his breath. His skin reddens. His veins bulge. Then he releases.

'I'm telling you,' he says breathlessly. 'I don't have it. I never put it on.'

Lady Melksham lowers her arm. 'Then where is it?'

'I don't know. It disappeared.'

'Do you know? I think I believe you. You wouldn't do anything to hurt your daughter.' She puts the Taser back onto the dressing table.

I almost sag to the floor in relief. Then suddenly the delivery guy bursts into the room.

'Mum, did you—' He breaks off and looks at me. 'That's Scarlet McCall!'

'Yes, Richard, we have established that,' says Lady Melksham.

'So it was you! You did it!' he says, looking at me in astonishment.

'Did what?' I ask, my blood chilling.

'You turned off the security system!' He tears his eyes away from me to Lady Melksham. 'I put the dogs away, but I wanted to check the CCTV, see if I could find out what spooked them. And the whole thing is off. I looked at the outside alarms, and they're off too.'

'I didn't touch them,' I say.

'No, she didn't do it,' says Lady Melksham, with a groan. Her forefinger flickers between Matt and herself. 'We checked the CCTV footage too, and must have somehow switched it all off. Did you switch it back on?'

Richard shoves his hands into his pockets. 'No!'

'Why ever not?' she demands.

'Because I had to put the jaguar back,' he says, lifting his head defiantly. 'The new one you bought . . . without telling me! Surely two was enough for studying behavioural patterns.'

'What are you talking about? What new jaguar?' says Lady Melksham.

Uh oh!

'I found one in the holding room,' he says. 'I took it

back into the zoo and left it there, while I got the keys to lock it up. I've just been back and it's gone.'

Lady Melksham stares at Richard. 'You saw a jaguar on the loose?' she asks, her words low and threatening.

My stomach dissolves.

'Yeah,' says Richard. 'When were you going to tell me you bought one?'

Lady Melksham turns to me. I can almost see her brain sifting through the facts. 'Oh my!' she says, her words chilling me to the bone.

I gulp. She's got it.

'How could I have been so stupid? I hadn't thought for one moment that your father would actually let his child touch the bracelet, let alone put it on. But he did. There's no way anyone could get into my house un-detected unless they transformed into an animal.'

She marches towards me.

'You're mad! She can't change into an animal,' shrieks Dad, struggling to free himself from the chair.

'But how can you transform if you haven't got the masks?' she continues, towering over me. Her eyes widen. 'You don't need them, do you?'

I scramble backwards before staggering to my feet.

'Leave her alone!' roars Dad.

Lady Melksham snatches the Taser. She points it at me, and then at Dad. 'Which one of you should I elec-trocute first?'

My insides explode. How dare she threaten Dad! I don't care who sees me change. My body warms and I relish the surging heat. What will I be? Will I peck them to death? Rip out their throats?

Everyone in the room screams, including Dad.

All three Melkshams turn white, frozen to the ground. Then Lady Melksham lunges towards me.

No freaking way! I lean back on my haunches and spring forward.

CHAPTER
TWENTY-SEVEN

I don't aim for Lady Melksham's body. I go for the stun gun instead. I tear it out of her hand, and bite down as hard as I can, but my teeth only scrape the surface. The Taser slips out of my grasp and falls to the floor.

'One of you, get her!' yells Lady Melksham.

Out of the corner of my eye, I see Richard frozen in shock. But Matt hurtles across the room to the stun gun lying on the carpet. I leap towards him. Our bodies slam. My claws rip through his T-shirt, piercing his shoulders. Matt crashes to the ground, his head smacking the wall, his eyes rolling backwards. I stand over him, inhaling the blood, licking my lips. I open my mouth.

People are shrieking but I don't care. I lower my head. Then I freeze. He didn't tackle me back on Dartmoor. He didn't stun Dad. Before I can change my mind, I jump off and race out of the room.

I run down the corridor, hurdle over the balustrade and land on all fours halfway down the staircase. Bounding down to the entrance hall, I hear footsteps pounding the floors above. They'll be here any minute. But I know what to do. I just hope Richard put the keys back.

I stare at my reflection in the window and my fur recedes. As soon as my fingers return, I yank open the door and run through the holding room. I burst into the zoo and head straight for the hook fastened to the aquarium. Yes! The keys are there. Sprinting over to the wildcat cage, I shove the key into the lock. I'm about to turn it, when I pause. What if they eat me?

The jaguars step away from the entrance of the cage. Do they understand what I'm doing?

Then Lady Melksham blasts into the room followed by Richard. Richard stares at me as if I'm a mutant.

Lady Melksham's eyes flicker to my hand. 'Don't be so stupid! They'll kill us all.'

'Only you,' I say.

'What? You think they won't touch you because you have the bracelet? They're animals. Dumb animals. They'll kill you too.'

'I'm willing to take that chance,' I say, sounding far braver than I feel.

'Scar!' she hisses.

'Only Dad calls me that!'

Lady Melksham rushes towards me, the Taser back

in her hand. How stupid was I? I should have taken it with me. She stops a metre away.

'Scarlet, this is on its highest setting, one I've never used before. Who knows what damage it will do?' says Lady Melksham. 'I don't want to, but I will use it. Step away from the cage.'

My wrist starts to strangle and I know I'm about to transform. That's not a bad thing. I can attack her. But I catch my reflection in the glass to the alligator's tank and the sensation stops. *Why did I look?* I'll have to stick to my original plan.

I turn the key.

Lady Melksham lunges forward and her finger hits the trigger. Out of instinct I drop to the floor. Electricity sizzles. I brace myself for pain, but to my astonishment, it's Lady Melksham who shrieks as the current slams into her. She sprawls across the central aisle, her body convulsing. My stomach lurches. The Taser must have backfired. Did I damage it with my teeth earlier? If jaguars can bite through skulls, what can they do to a Taser?

I clamber to my feet as the door to the wildcat cage eases open. I turn to see a jaguar edging it ajar with his nose. My heart pounds and I swallow. Animals smell fear. I must stink.

'Scarlet, don't move,' says Richard, in a loud whisper from the edge of the room. 'I'm going to get another gun. I'll be back as soon as I can.'

Is he trying to help me?

Richard turns slowly around and walks carefully through the holding room, when two jaguars leap out of the cage. They don't even look at me. They bound over Lady Melksham's twitching body and hurtle through the open doorway.

There's an almighty roar, followed by a blood-curdling scream—Richard. Then there's silence. I start to shake. I can't stop. Richard was helping me and now look what's happened. What have I done?

Oh God! What if the jaguars find Dad? He's tied up and can't escape.

Without a second thought, I jump over Lady Melksham and race into the holding room. The sight of Richard's body lying on the floor stops me in my tracks. He's covered in blood and bite marks, but to my relief, his chest rises up and down. He's still alive, but he'll need a hospital soon.

I clench my fists. I can't let those jaguars hurt Dad.

Tearing up the stairs, two at a time, I rush through the corridor into his room. Dad's sitting in the chair with his back to me. Matt is where I left him, still out cold. The jaguars are nowhere to be seen.

'Dad, are you OK?' I say, my voice breathless. I grab the picklock from the dressing table and drop to my knees.

'Scar, Scar,' Dad mumbles. His face is pale and his eyes are wild.

'It's all right, I'm going to get you out of here,' I say.

'You . . . you became a leopard.'

'I was a jaguar. I promise I'll explain everything later. But right now, I've got to get you out of here.' The handcuffs come apart easily.

'A jaguar?' he repeats, shaking his head from side to side.

I fumble with the padlock at his ankles. 'It's because of the bracelet. The one that sank into my skin.'

'It really happened then? The gold didn't disintegrate?'

I look up and nod. 'Yes, it really happened.'

Dad frowns. 'Lady Melksham's been quizzing me about its powers. She's been cutting my wrist, searching for it.' He holds up his hands.

'I know she has,' I say, through gritted teeth. 'But don't worry. She won't be doing it again.'

The lock springs open and I unwrap the chains from Dad's legs. I help him to his feet but he seems unsteady.

I look Dad straight in the eyes. 'Listen, I know you've been through a lot, but there's something you have to do for me. It's important.'

Dad looks at me dazedly.

'There's a car—a silver car—about a mile away from here, on the outside of the perimeter wall. If you go down the driveway to the gates, walk along the wall, you'll come to it. The CCTV is off, so you don't have to worry about getting caught on camera. But get there as fast as you can.' An image of two jaguars flickers into my mind. They could be in the house, in the garden, or prowling the countryside. Dad needs something to protect himself. I yank a set of grappling hooks out of

184

my rucksack and shove them into his hands. 'There may be wild animals on the loose. If you have to, use these.'

'Wild animals?' Dad mutters, looking vacant. Like he's coming out of anaesthetic.

I put my arm through his and escort him out of the room, making sure I shut the door. I don't want any animals attacking Matt.

We walk slower than I'd like, but Dad refuses to hurry. We climb down the stairs into the entrance hall.

'Dad, there's a boy called Ethan waiting for you in the car,' I say.

Dad looks at me blankly. I'm not sure how much he's taking in.

'Ethan's my friend. He's helped me, and he's going to help you, but he can't drive. I need you to drive the car back here, and meet me outside the house, by the front door. Do you understand?'

Dad doesn't respond.

'I said, *do you understand*?' I ask again. 'Dad. *Dad!* I need to know I can trust you. I need to know you'll do exactly as I say.'

A spark ignites in his eyes. Maybe hearing his own words defogged his brain. But he doesn't nod. Instead he shakes his head.

'I'm not leaving you here,' he says. 'You've got to come with me now.'

'No! There are things I have to do.'

'Then I'll stay.'

'You can't. You need to find Ethan.' I look at him imploringly. 'I . . . I can't be worrying about you while I—'

Dad's jaw clenches.

'Please!' I say again.

At last Dad nods. 'All right. I'll be back here, as soon as I can . . . with the car and with Ethan.'

So he was listening!

I watch him walk out of the front door and down the driveway.

'Oh, Dad,' I yell. 'Don't get out of the car. Don't let Ethan either.'

He lifts his arm into the air and I know he's heard me.

But will they do as I say? That's the question.

CHAPTER TWENTY-EIGHT

I run straight for the museum. As soon as I open the door, the smell of incense hits me. Trying to ignore it, I grab the jaguar mask and shove it into my rucksack. There's no way they're keeping this after what they've done to Dad. Then I head to the item I need the most.

The yellow powder in the brown pouch looks like nothing, but if I'm right and it actually works, it might save us. I clasp it in my hand when I hear a voice.

'Planning on stealing everything then? Not just my bracelet.'

I step out from behind the cabinet to see Lady Melksham marching towards me. Her hair, no longer perfect, sticking out in all directions. Her eyeliner and mascara drip down her face and her lipstick is smeared.

She looks grotesque, a gargoyle. But it's the long brown gun in her hands that takes my breath away.

'Oh don't look so scared,' she says. 'It's only a tranquilizer gun. The darts won't kill you. They'll only put you to sleep. I used them when I shot my pets—the alligators—in Mexico.'

'You *shot* them?' I croak.

She points the gun in my direction. 'The arrows tore through their hard scales. I wonder what they'll do to the flesh of a girl?'

I stare at her in horror. She has a wild look in her eyes, as if deranged. Was she always like this? Or has the electric shock unhinged her? I guess it doesn't matter. I just need to escape.

I look down at my wrist. Come on! I wait for my skin to tighten. Nothing happens. I clench every muscle in my body, waiting for the heat to take over. Again nothing. I try to breathe deeply but my lungs seem blocked, filled with smoke. *Body—change!* I cry silently. Let me be a jaguar, an eagle. Hey, let me be an alligator. At least the darts won't cause too much harm.

'What are you doing? You're going red,' says Lady Melksham, stepping closer. 'Oh—you're trying to transform. But you can't. Why not?'

I have no earthly idea, but I do know I have to get out of here. And I'll have to get out of here as a girl.

Lady Melksham looks at the pouch in my hand. 'You do realize that powder won't work. It's just crushed stone. I should know, I tested it on my boys.'

'Maybe you didn't use it correctly,' I say, slowly stepping sideways.

Lady Melksham bursts out laughing. 'Oh I see. You know more about Aztec artefacts than I do?'

I shove the pouch into my jeans back pocket, and take another three steps sideways until I'm standing behind the glass cabinet.

'Have you spent the last twenty years uncovering lost sculptures? Have you spent your life travelling to Mexico?' Lady Melksham takes a few side steps too until she's opposite me, her eyes gleaming hysterically. She prods her finger in my direction. 'Well . . . have you?'

Using all of my strength, I shove the cabinet forward. It topples towards her. Lady Melksham screams and drops the gun. She tries to run but the cabinet slams her to the ground. Glass shatters. Shields, spears, pots fall on top of her, all around her.

I run for the doorway, my shoes crunching the glass. I hurtle down the corridor. Somewhere in my brain I register an open door to my left, but I don't have time to think about it. Lady Melksham is behind me.

'You can't escape me!' she shouts.

At least, I think it's her shouting. Her voice is no longer clipped. It's rough, flat, Lancastrian, and furious. Her footsteps quicken. Why wasn't she crushed? Can nothing stop her?

I reach the balustrade overhanging the sweeping staircase. I'm going to have to risk it. Grabbing onto the railings, I swing my legs over and career through the air.

Somehow, I land on my feet halfway down the staircase. I give myself a shake, not quite believing my legs aren't broken, then run down the remaining steps. I know I shouldn't waste time turning around, but I can't help it. I twist my head to see Lady Melksham leap over the railings, copying me.

'You're mine!' she shrieks.

She soars through the air. Her feet miss the steps. Her ankles twist and she rolls past me, head over heels. Her body crashes to the bottom, her legs at a funny angle. I can't tell if she's alive or dead.

All at once I hear a roar. There's no way I can leave her to the jaguars, so I grab Lady Melksham's hand and drag her across the floor into the holding room. I'm grateful she's so thin. Richard is in the same place, a pool of blood beside him. His breathing's more laboured and I know I'll have to call for an ambulance soon.

I open the door to the zoo. Against the silence of the house, the animal screeches are deafening. I pull Lady Melksham into the jaguar cage and let go.

Rubbing my arms, I head back to the holding room and grab Richard's hands. In his condition, he shouldn't be moved, but I can't leave him here. I pull him gently. He groans . . . but he doesn't budge a millimetre.

Suddenly my wrist aches, my temperature rises. Seriously? *Now* I'm changing? But I don't fight it. I must be transforming for a reason.

Soon I'm on all fours. The smell of Richard's blood wafts up my nose, but I refuse to eat him. Instead I grab the end of his trouser leg with my teeth and pull. I'm far stronger now. He slides across the floor, leaving a trail of blood behind. I heave him into the jaguars' cage and lie down, catching my breath, gathering my energy. I need to get Matt from upstairs.

Then I hear uneven footsteps. Deep breathing. I leap to my feet, spin around and see Matt limping down the aisle.

'What have you done to them?' he cries, his face red with fury.

CHAPTER TWENTY-NINE

'It wasn't me!' I want to tell him, but a low rumble comes from the back of my throat.

'I've—I've never shot an animal before,' says Matt, his voice trembling.

I look at his hand, expecting to see a Taser. My pulse spikes. He's got a real gun.

'This is Rich's,' he says, holding the gun out in front of him. He clutches his wrist with his other hand, trying to keep the gun steady. It's not working. 'Rich used it as a warning shot when we raided your house. I'm—I'm not going to use it as a warning shot.'

I watch in horror as his finger presses down. I have no choice. I pounce. My claws crash into his chest, pushing him backwards as he pulls the trigger. A bullet rockets into the ceiling. Plaster falls on both of us as we crash to the ground, me on top of him. I leap off, not wanting to crush his lungs. But to my horror and disbelief, he clambers back to his feet. Can nothing stop this boy? He's just like his mum.

I look him straight in the eyes, willing him to understand. *'I DO NOT WANT TO HURT YOU!'*

He seems to nod before bending down. Has he understood? He sweeps something off the floor and waves it in my direction. No, I don't think so! It's the Taser his mum dropped.

'I wouldn't use that if I were you!' I say, in a low growl.

'Scared, are you?' he says, his voice trembling even more. Blood oozes from his chest.

'Don't use it!' I growl louder.

He lowers the Taser towards me. I scrabble away. It backfired last time. But will it do it again?

'This is for Mum and Rich,' he shouts, pressing the button.

Electricity shoots out, hitting Matt straight in the face. His scream freezes my blood. He's thrown backwards, his body soaring through the air before smacking to the ground. I wait, watching. Will he get up? Then I smell burning flesh and see his body convulse.

I rush towards him. *Please don't be dead.* Then he gasps for breath, and relief floods through me. But I have no time to relax.

I drag his twitching body next to Richard's. My eyes dart from one unconscious person to the next. With a mixture of relief and despair, I pad out of the cage and gaze at the glass in the aquarium.

Two alligators watch me; their magnificent jaws open, hissing. But I ignore them. Instead I stare at the dark reflection and feel warmth spread through my body. My limbs melt and soon it's a girl staring back at me. Her eyes look haunted; as though she's seen things she hopes to forget one day.

The screech of an eagle jolts my brain awake. Is it Itzca wanting Richard? All I know is that I haven't finished yet. I fish out the brown pouch from my jeans and return to the wildcat cage.

Kneeling beside Lady Melksham, I whisper, 'You told me this doesn't work. I hope to God you were lying.'

I grab a pinch of yellow powder between my finger and thumb. Thankfully Lady Melksham's mouth is already open. I place the powder on her tongue and it starts to sizzle. I rush over to Matt. His mouth is closed. With a squirming stomach, I prise his lips open and drop some powder onto his tongue. I then move onto Richard. I can hear cracks and pops of the powder in each of their mouths, and it dawns on me that all the animals have fallen silent, as if they realize the importance of this moment.

Stuffing the pouch back into my pocket, I stand up and take a deep breath. Then in a loud, solemn voice, I say, 'Melkshams—you will not remember my dad or mum, Daniel McCall or Tallulah McCall. You will not remember Scarlet McCall. You've never met them and you've never heard of them. You've studied the Aztecs for a long time, and you've heard of the Legend of Achcauhtli and the bracelet. But you do not believe it. You think it's a made-up story. You do not steal Aztec artefacts. You've collected them over the years but now you want to dedicate them to a museum in Mexico. You've also collected wild animals as a hobby, but now you know they should be in a safari park.'

I wrack my brains. Anything else? I don't want to miss something out.

'Oh . . . and you can't stand fur coats. You were given some as a gift and you can't wait to destroy them.'

I think that's everything. I just hope it works, otherwise when they wake up they're going to be after Dad and me . . . and the bracelet . . . and more animals . . .

I step out of the cage and close the door to find the key still in the lock. My eyes linger on each of the Melkshams. They're a terrible, twisted family, but still . . . I don't want them to die. I lock them in, and drop the keys just inside the jaguar cage, well in reach of any rescuers. I'm hoping they'll assume Lady Melksham locked herself in for her own safety.

Turning around, I look at the other animals. I could free them now, but I'm not sure how long they'd survive. It's better if they stay here until people come for them.

Now I need a phone. I'm sure I spotted one earlier hanging on the wall in the entrance hall. Returning to the room, I find it straight away. And with trembling fingers I dial 999.

'Which emergency service do you require?' says the operator.

'I need all of them,' I reply in clipped tones. 'There's been . . . some accidents. There are two people who need ambulances straight away.'

'Are they breathing?'

'Just about.'

The operator starts asking questions but I talk over her knowing that the call is being recorded. 'They are in a big house in the Lake District. The postcode is LA23 5ZS. You definitely need ambulances. But you also need the RSPCA. There are monkeys, alligators, eagles, and wolves in cages that need to be rehoused. But there are jaguars on the loose.'

The woman stops asking questions. There's silence.

'I repeat there are monkeys, alligators, eagles, and wolves in cages that need—'

'Is this a prank call?' demands the operator.

'No,' I say, my accent slipping.

I can almost hear the operator snarl. 'I cannot believe you're wasting time on this precious phone line with a prank—'

'And I can't believe you don't believe me!' I interrupt. My body grows hot and I want to shout at her. I want to scream that the ambulance must come now. I open my mouth to tell her what I think . . . when a deep terrifying roar rips out from the back of my throat.

'Was that a lion?' yelps the operator, just as I hear the sound of a car approaching.

I clear my throat and my fake voice say, 'That was a jaguar. You need to come quickly. I'm going to lock myself in a cage for safety.' Then I hang up.

Looking out of the window, I see a car pulling up on the driveway. The passenger door opens and Ethan jumps onto the gravel.

'Scarlet, you did it!' he yells. But he's not looking in my direction. He's looking to his left.

I open the door and my heart stops. A jaguar is standing five metres away from Ethan, lying on its haunches, ready to pounce. Without thinking, I hurtle across the driveway, barrelling Ethan into the car. I sense rather than see the jaguar leap towards me. Twisting in mid-air, I transform faster than ever before. I meet the jaguar head on, our claws ripping through each other's fur.

I'm bigger than she is, and instinctively want to be boss. I bite the back of her neck, piercing her skin. Screams fly from the car. The jaguar tries to wrench herself free, but my teeth clamp together. Blood drips down my mouth. Then I freeze.

The jaguar struggles in my mouth and this time I open my jaws, releasing her. She hurtles away, terrified. She doesn't know what I am.

I'm not sure what I am either.

CHAPTER THIRTY

Still there are screams. I turn to face the car, and in the reflection of the window, I see blood dripping from my fangs. I wait as my body transforms back into a human and then open the door. Wiping the jaguar blood onto the back of my hand, I climb inside. The screaming stops. But the silence is louder.

Dad starts the engine and pulls away from the house. No one speaks.

Finally, as we reach the edge of the Lake District, Ethan says, 'Thanks for saving my life.' He speaks softly but his words shatter the silence.

'Do you want to tell me what the hell is going on?' says Dad.

He pulls over, so Ethan and I can swap seats. Then I tell him everything. Well . . . almost everything.

*

Halfway home, we stop at the same motorway services we'd used on the way. We park at a deserted spot, and Ethan and I start cleaning the Ford Focus. Dad, meanwhile, looks up its registration plate to work out who the owners are.

'I'll buy them an expensive present in a week, and have it delivered to their house anonymously,' he says.

Then he stops us from cleaning the car too well. We get rid of fingerprints, but leave soggy chips and wrappers in the footwell.

'You want to make it look like teenagers stole it,' he says.

'Teenagers did steal it,' I reply.

Dad throws me half a smile. 'OK—you want to make it look like teenagers without a noble purpose stole it.'

'You think we're noble?'

'Scar, I think what you did was amazing. You stole a car without being detected. You got into a fortress and rescued me. Gave me my insulin. You change into animals and don't seem completely freaked out about it.'

'I was. Believe me—I was.'

'Plus to top it off, you managed to get some Aztec artefacts back.' He plants his hands on my shoulders. 'I've never been prouder of you.'

I feel bigger, stronger, taller, as I stare at Dad in wonder. He's proud of me. He's really proud of me.

'Scar, you were a complete pro,' he continues. 'And you're only thirteen. Your mother was fifteen when your Grandpa started teaching her.'

My look of wonder changes to one of shock. 'Grandpa taught her?'

'I'll tell you another time,' says Dad, slinging his arm around me. 'Come on, Pro. We better get going.'

We grab our stuff and lug it over to the hotel car park on the other side of the service station where we find Dad's Ford Fiesta.

I jump into the passenger seat, Dad's words still dancing in my ears, and Ethan climbs into the back. Dad fills up the car with petrol and soon the lights on the side of the road are whizzing by. Ethan starts snoring, but there's no way I can sleep. Dad puts on some music, and fiddles with the settings so that it's louder in the back of the car than in the front.

'We need to talk, without someone overhearing,' he says.

'Ethan can listen.'

'No, he can't!'

'But he helped me. He helped *us*! If he hadn't hacked into your laptop, you'd still be tied up. He's the one who found the plans of Lady Melksham's house.' I pause. 'Why do you have plans of her house?'

'Because I burgled it.'

'You what?' I say, bolting upright in my seat.

'I burgled it. Looking back, I should have realized what a cunning woman she was.'

I say nothing, waiting for him to continue.

'Seven years ago your mother and I were employed to get back an Austrian painting, a Gustav Klimt. It was

200

stolen during the Second World War and thought to be hanging in a house in the Lake District. Can you guess which house?'

'Lady Melksham's,' I say. 'So you knew she was a thief back then? But you still worked for her.'

'Hang on a minute,' says Dad. 'We researched the house—got plans from the planning office, added our own information, such as the location of security cameras and alarms.'

'Were the animals there? And all the Aztec artefacts?'

'No, she didn't have any of those things then, or if she did, she kept them somewhere else. But she did have the Austrian painting. It was a straight in-and-out job. Your mother and I took the painting without setting off any alarms, and I know we weren't caught on camera. So we went to meet our client, the rightful owner, at the rendezvous point. But when we got there, Lady Melksham was there too.'

'It was a trap?'

Dad shakes his head. 'It was a test. Lady Melksham wanted to know whether we were as good as she'd been told. As you can imagine, we passed. She couldn't believe we managed to get past her security. Since then she's added dogs, as well as pulled files from the planning office. I've had to link her house to Google Earth to keep tabs on her.'

'Why would you keep tabs on her?'

'I keep tabs on all my clients.' Dad squeezes the steering wheel. 'Lady Melksham told us this story about how she was trying to get artefacts back to Mexico. We checked her out and it all seemed legit.'

I sit back in my seat, thinking about what Dad's just told me, when another question worms its way into my head.

'Dad,' I say, uneasily. 'Lady Melksham said that you stole from a museum. Is that true?'

His foot slips off the accelerator.

'I'm guessing it is then.' My stomach twists. 'Did . . . did Mum do it with you?'

'Oh God, no!' says Dad, shaking his head.

I feel slightly relieved.

'It was after she died,' he says. 'She would never have let me. She was the one who chose most of the jobs, did the checks.'

She did? I always assumed Dad was in charge.

'So . . . why did you steal from a museum?' I ask, finally.

Dad sighs. 'Scar, you're like your mother. You see things in black and white, when there are so many shades.'

I remain silent, expecting him to give me a reason. But he doesn't. Instead he clears his throat. 'Now it's my turn to ask you a question. How badly were the Melkshams hurt? You said they were electrocuted and attacked by jaguars, but are they still able to talk? Will they be able to send the police around to our house or turn up themselves? What I really want to know is—is our house still compromised? Do we need to go somewhere else?'

I think of the brown pouch of yellow powder in my

back pocket—probably getting squashed. Should I tell him about it? But I can't. I've got plans for it . . .

'I think we'll be all right for at least a day,' I say. 'The Melkshams are pretty messed up. And Lady Melksham told me that if you use the Taser on its highest setting, it plays with your memory.'

'That's good,' says Dad, obviously believing my lie.

I feel a slight shiver. It's strange knowing more than he does. But I give myself a shake. 'So if they do say anything to the police, it probably won't make much sense. That should give us enough time to pack up our house and leave properly. Anyway, we have to take Ethan home.'

'And he won't say anything?'

I think of the yellow powder again. 'No, he won't say a thing.'

Dad rubs his forehead. 'Scar, you've thought of everything. It appears that my little apprentice has all grown up.'

I try to smile. 'Thank you, master.'

'But I do think we should stay at Nagimuru's house just in case. It will be safer. He's away—visiting relatives at the moment. We can keep tabs on our own house from there.'

I nod, when suddenly Dad pulls onto the hard shoulder.

'What are you doing?' I ask.

'How would you like to be my partner?' he says.

'What?'

'A fully fledged partner, like your mum was. You've

really proven yourself. The way you've thought on your feet, scaled walls, picked locks. Plus with your new found abilities, the way you can transform into birds or cats, you'll be able to get into houses undetected.'

'Are you serious?'

Dad switches on the indoor light and I glance behind to see if it's woken Ethan. He remains fast asleep.

'Yes,' says Dad. 'Think of the jobs we could do. We could do so many more—possibly one a week.'

His eyes are wide, shining brightly.

'But Dad, you've just been kidnapped.'

'You know what they say. If you fall off a horse, get straight back on.'

'Don't you want some time off? I kind of assumed you would.'

'And miss the thrill? Miss the buzz?' he says, rubbing his hands.

I don't say anything.

'Maybe I've asked too soon. You've been through a lot. We'll talk about it tomorrow.'

'Yeah . . . OK,' I say.

Dad switches off the light and starts the car again. I lean my head against the window. What is wrong with me? If Dad had asked me this a week ago, I would have jumped at the opportunity. I would have said yes and we'd be discussing plans. I love the fact that he thinks I'm good enough. I love the fact that he's so proud of me. But—and it's a big but—something doesn't feel right. I just can't put my finger on what it is.

CHAPTER
THIRTY-ONE

By the time we pull into the drive, the sun is peeping over Mr Nagimuru's rooftop. Dad switches off the engine, and I turn around in my seat.

'We're back,' I say.

Ethan's face is squashed up against the window, his eyes shut, drool on his chin, hair sticking out in all directions. He'd be horrified if he knew what he looked like. He makes a small grunt but doesn't move.

'I said, we're back,' I say louder, reaching over and shaking his knee.

Ethan bolts upright. He stares around with a dazed expression and my lips twitch. I bet he thought he was tucked up in bed.

Dad climbs out of the car and opens Ethan's door.

'Ethan, thank you for everything,' he says. 'I really

appreciate what you've done for me and Scar. She obviously trusts you, which means I trust you.'

Ethan smiles and my insides squeal.

'But, let me say this,' says Dad, his voice suddenly deepening. He leans in closer. 'If you *ever* do anything to spoil that trust, your life will become very difficult. I *will* make sure of it.'

Ethan's jaw drops, and I stare at Dad in horror.

'Well, thanks again,' says Dad, before turning around and disappearing into Mr Nagimuru's house.

For a moment there's silence.

'Did your Dad mean that?' whispers Ethan, finally.

'No, of course he didn't,' I say, but I'm not convinced. I've never seen Dad act like that before. 'Come on, let me take you to your gran's.'

We grab our rucksacks and I pick up Dad's laptop too. I walk Ethan back to number four. He looks terrified, and I bet he's still thinking about Dad. I stop at the edge of his front garden.

'We do really appreciate what you did. We couldn't have done it without you.'

Ethan snorts.

'It's true,' I say. Then hesitate. 'Listen Ethan, I was wondering if I could ask you one more favour. Would you look after my bag and Dad's laptop?'

'Don't you want them? Doesn't your Dad want that back?' says Ethan, looking slightly fearful.

'I don't want them now. I want them later,' I say. 'If the Melkshams wake up and remember everything, they're going to come looking for Dad and me. They know where we live. They'll want their stuff back.'

Ethan's eyes widen. 'They won't just want their stuff back. They'll want revenge.'

'I'm not so bothered about that. I can handle them,' I say, lifting my wrist into the air. 'It's just . . . I don't want them having any of this stuff. They don't deserve it.'

'But what about you?' says Ethan. 'Don't you want to stay at mine?'

'I can't leave Dad.'

Ethan sighs heavily. 'All right, I'll take them.'

I hand him the laptop and rucksack, and watch him go into his gran's house. Then I head for home. There's something I have to get before I go to Mr Nagimuru's. For all I know, the powder didn't work. The Melkshams might have woken up and be on their way here right now.

I push open the front door to our house and step over broken glass. I hurry upstairs to my room and find it straight away. The photo of Mum and me. There's no way I'm parting with this again.

My skin crawls as I look around my room. The Melkshams did this. They caused the mess, kidnapped, used Tasers, real guns. And suddenly I know exactly what's bothering me about becoming Dad's equal. For I can see him back in the car, asking me to be his partner. His eyes were gleaming, almost manic. He was so excited at the thought of doing more burglaries, of using my powers to help. He reminded me of . . . Lady Melksham.

I glance down at the photo in my hand. Dad said Mum was the one who used to do the checks. Did she rein Dad in? Do I need to rein him in?

I pat my jeans pocket, making sure I still have the brown pouch, before heading over to Mr Nagimuru's. His front door is unlocked.

'Dad!' I call, stepping inside.

I hear nothing.

'Dad!' I call again, louder this time.

Still nothing.

My heart begins to pound. Did the powder not work? Did the Melkshams follow us and find Dad here? My brain goes into overdrive as I hurtle from room to room. Dad's nowhere to be found on the ground floor, so I rush upstairs. I hear a snuffle.

Whisking open the nearest door, I almost burst out laughing with relief. Dad is lying fully dressed, fast asleep on a double bed. I don't blame him for falling asleep after all that he's been through. But thinking of the fear I felt when I couldn't find him, makes me all the more determined.

Pulling out the brown pouch, I tiptoe across the room and kneel beside the bed. Dad doesn't even stir. I take a pinch of yellow powder. It may simply be crushed sand, and the Melkshams are on their way here already. But I'm going to give it a try.

Thankfully Dad's mouth is open and it's easy to drop the powder onto his tongue. It crackles and sizzles.

'Dad,' I whisper, not daring to speak in a loud voice.

'You don't know anything about a gold and turquoise bracelet. You don't know anything about the legend of Achcauhtli or me transforming into animals. You don't know the Melkshams. You've never done a job for them. You know nothing about Aztec artefacts.'

I stand up and Dad rolls over. I open my mouth, preparing to tell him that he knows nothing about cat burglary; that his only job is for Mr Higgs. But I can't do it. Cat burglary is Dad's life. And I'm pretty sure he thinks he's helping people. It's not just for the money . . . it can't be . . .

Anyway, if he stopped cat burglary, what would we have to talk about?

And so I only have a few things left to say. 'Dad, we were burgled. They weren't looking for us, it was just bad luck, and they only found some money—it wasn't much. You thought we should stay at Mr Nagimuru's, though, just to be on the safe side. Oh . . . and you fell over on a training exercise and got pretty bruised.'

I walk out of the room and open another door, grateful there's a bed inside. Flopping onto the patchwork duvet, I plan to stay awake in case the Melkshams come. But as I lie fully clothed, listening out for cars, it's hard to keep my eyes open. Just before I fall asleep, one thought slips through my mind.

Let the powder work . . .

CHAPTER
THIRTY-TWO

'Scar, wake up.'

I open my eyes to see Dad looming over me, a cup of tea in his hand. Memories of the previous night come flooding back. Did the powder work? Or are the Melkshams on their way?

'I tried knocking but you were fast asleep,' says Dad. 'I don't know what's wrong with us. We both slept in. It's almost two o'clock.'

'I had a late night. I couldn't put my book down,' I say, watching him, gauging his reaction.

Dad puts the tea onto the bedside table. 'Must have been a good book. You didn't even bother getting changed for bed.'

I almost explode with relief. He doesn't remember. That means the Melkshams won't remember either. 'I forgot to bring my pyjamas over,' I say.

'Me too,' says Dad. 'I've just been back to our house. I've started the clean up.'

'Do . . . do you have any idea who did it?' I ask, sitting up. 'Why we were burgled?'

Dad shakes his head. 'By the looks of it, it was an opportunistic burglar. They took some money, but not much.'

'They didn't find the safe then?'

'Have you seen the state of the house? They weren't professionals. They weren't us.'

Whoa—that powder's good.

Dad rubs his forehead. 'After your cup of tea, I think we should both go back over. I want to carry on, and I imagine you want to start on your bedroom. I know how you like to have it perfectly tidy.'

'Actually Dad, do you mind if I go for a run first? I need to clear my head. I'll help you with the rest of the house then, too.'

'Yeah, sure. The mess isn't going anywhere,' says Dad. 'Why don't you scale some trees while you're at it? You could do with the practice. I've got a job coming up. If you show promise, I might let you do a little more than carry the tools.'

My stomach drops. I force a smile to my face and nod. Of course—Dad doesn't remember how I scaled the Harlington house, or how I got the bracelet on my own. All that pride and admiration he had for me has gone. Vanished.

'I'll see you later,' I mumble.

'Cheer up,' says Dad. 'We'll soon sort out the mess, and your room will look as good as new.'

I clamber over the hedge into number four's garden, heading straight for the oak tree. I grab one of the nodules sticking out from the trunk when someone, somewhere says the name, 'Lady Melksham.'

I freeze.

'Apparently Lady Melksham's jaguars escaped from their cages in the middle of last night,' says the voice. 'Nobody can quite work out how they managed it.'

My fingers release the nodule and I step out from under the tree. Who's speaking? Then I look at the giant television in Ethan's gran's living room. My heart seems to freeze and then pounds like crazy. Lady Melksham fills the screen. She's covered in bruises and blood, and has a grey blanket draped over her shoulders. Two paramedics are helping her into an ambulance.

A journalist in the corner of the screen says, 'At some point, the animals attacked Lady Melksham and her two sons. They managed to get to safety though, by locking themselves in a cage, a jaguar cage. The RSPCA found the jaguars wandering the hillside. It's lucky they didn't attack any farms.'

'Do we know what other animals Lady Melksham kept?' asks the off-screen voice.

'We do,' says the journalist, clasping his hands together. 'She kept wolves, monkeys, eagles, and alligators.'

'What's happening to them?' asks the off-screen voice.

'The RSPCA are looking at rehousing them at safari parks around the country,' says the journalist.

I think of the larger enclosures the creatures will have now, and my heart lifts.

'Do you have any idea why Lady Melksham kept such animals in the first place?'

'Lady Melksham is passionate about the Aztec culture. She's donated thousands and thousands of pounds towards preserving Aztec antiquities in Mexico and she is regarded as a hero out there.'

I stare at the screen. She is?

'Jaguars, wolves, monkeys, eagles, and alligators were revered by the Aztecs and it is assumed Lady Melksham kept them for that reason,' continues the journalist.

'And how is Lady Melksham?'

'Her injuries are said not to be serious. She—oh could you wait a moment please? I'm getting some news.' The journalist places his hand to his earpiece. His face falls and in a solemn voice he says, 'I'm sorry to tell you that one of her sons has just been rushed into intensive care.'

My blood turns to ice. Which one?

'We can tell you that it is fourteen-year-old Matthew Melksham.'

A photo of a messy-haired boy fills the screen. I stagger backwards. Fourteen. Just a year older than me. The same age as Ethan.

'Was he attacked by an animal?' asks the off-screen voice.

'Apparently he has scratch marks on his chest, but it seems that a faulty Taser may also be involved. He will be—'

Suddenly the image on the screen changes, and I'm staring at two women chatting in a pub. Where's Lady Melksham gone? Where's the journalist?

Then I notice Ethan's gran standing near the sofa, a steaming cup in one hand and a remote control in the other. She's changed channel to a soap opera. My jaw clenches. I dash back under the tree. I'll have to watch the news in Ethan's room.

Within seconds I'm at the top of the oak. Ethan's window is open, and I guess he's expecting me. But, when I peer into the room, he isn't sat at his computer, like I thought he'd be. He's leaning over his bed, scrutinizing the Aztec mask.

'About time,' he says, not looking up, as I swing into the room.

'What are you doing?' I ask.

'A bit of research. I've been doing it all day. I haven't slept.' He finally looks up. Dark rings surround his eyes.

'Couldn't you sleep?' I say.

'I didn't want to. I've been looking out for the Melkshams. See if they turned up.'

'We were at Mr Nagimuru's. I told you I could handle them,' I say, waving my wrist.

'You might have needed a warning,' he says. 'Anyway,

how's your dad? In fact, how are you? You look deathly pale.'

Whoa! I must look bad if that's coming from Ethan! I swallow. There's a sour taste in my mouth. 'One of Lady Melksham's sons is in intensive care. The younger one.'

'Oh no!' Ethan closes his eyes.

'He has complications caused by a faulty Taser. The Taser I made faulty.'

Ethan's eyes flash open and he walks straight towards me. 'You better not be blaming yourself. No one made him use that Taser.'

'How do you know what happened?'

'I heard you tell your dad last night. If you hadn't done something, he would have killed you. You did it in self-defence.'

'I don't know. He . . . he didn't like hurting anything. I think I drove him to it.'

'How can you say that? He kept animals in cages long before you came along. He helped kidnap your dad. He tried to get you.'

'He didn't seem that bad. He's only a kid.'

'He's older than you!' Ethan grabs hold of my shoulders. 'Scarlet, over the last few days, you've been awesome. The things you've done—I don't know anyone else who could do half of those.'

His words remind me of Dad's and I smile thinly. Soon Ethan won't remember any of this either. I step backwards, out of his grip.

'I was going to ask you to put the news on your

computer, but I think I should tell you something first.' I pause. I'm not sure why I'm telling him this, especially since he won't remember, but I feel like I owe him. 'Dad was really wrong about Lady Melksham. What if he's wrong about his other clients? So I've decided I'm going to do the checks for him, like my Mum used to. And we'll only target people who've already stolen.'

'Will he let you? Won't he want to do the checks himself?'

'I might have to do it . . . secretly. Now I know the passwords to his laptop.'

Ethan smiles 'Or you could always threaten him as a jaguar.'

'Actually I can't do that,' I say, shaking my head.

'I didn't really expect you too! I was joking. It's only me you threaten.'

'No, really I can't. Dad doesn't know I can transform. I wiped his memory last night. He doesn't know anything about the bracelet, the Melkshams. In fact he doesn't know anything about Aztec artefacts.' I stop talking, for the smile has dropped from Ethan's face. His mouth is open. His eyes are wide.

'You did what?' he whispers.

'I'm a risk. There are people out there who will want to use my powers for bad things, wrong things. Dad will be safer not knowing. So I wiped his memory.'

'How?'

Reaching for my back pocket, I pull out the brown pouch, and tell Ethan about the powers of the yellow dust—how it worked on the Melkshams, how it worked on Dad.

He stares at the powder, then steps back, his eyes flashing with rage. 'You're planning to use it on me, aren't you?'

CHAPTER
THIRTY-THREE

I feel my cheeks flush. 'I'm going to get you to wipe Dad's laptop first, get rid of everything about the Aztecs.'

Ethan doesn't take his eyes off the powder. 'Don't I have to be asleep?'

'I'm going to knock you out.'

'What?'

'But you won't remember,' I say, quickly.

'Oh, *that's* all right then!' snaps Ethan, glaring at me. His lip curls. 'I cannot believe you're going to use that on me after everything I've done for you.'

'Ethan, don't take it personally. I've used it on Dad too.'

'Don't take it personally? You're about to wipe my memory—tamper with my brain. Of course I'm taking it personally.' He rubs the back of his neck. 'What have I done for you not to trust me? I haven't told anyone about what you can do. And I've helped you in every way I can.'

'I know,' I say, my insides squirming.

'What can I do to prove myself?'

'You don't have to do anything. It's just . . .' my words break off. Then I take a deep breath. 'I'm not used to this. I'm not used to relying on someone else; letting someone else help me. Normally it's just me and Dad.'

'But it doesn't have to be. And your dad can't help you now, not with the bracelet anyway. Or with your shape changes. I can help you when you transform into a monkey or an alligator or a wolf. Because you will one day, won't you? And I can help you do the checks on your dad's clients. You know you can't do techy things on your own.'

I squeeze my eyes shut. It's been amazing having Ethan as a friend. He hasn't let me down once . . . and I could do with someone's help. I open my eyes and put the pouch back in my jeans pocket. I only hope I'm not going to regret this. 'I trust you,' I whisper.

'You do?' says Ethan, a grin beginning to appear on his face.

I nod.

He cocks his head. 'I don't suppose you'll throw that powder away then?'

With a small smile, I say, 'No! I never know when I might need it.'

Ethan stretches out his arms, and flexes his mus-cles—what he has of them. 'Just so you know—I wouldn't have let you knock me out anyway. I can take on a jaguar or an eagle.'

'I'm sure you can!' I say, and we both burst out laughing, when all at once I remember something. 'Ethan, now that we're going to be working together, I need to ask you. I think I've worked out when I transform—it's not just when I want something—it's when my life is threatened. But last night, Lady Melksham was about to kill me. I needed my powers more than ever, but they didn't work. Why would that be?'

'Maybe there's something that stops them from—'

Suddenly a siren blares. Ethan falls silent. My blood chills.

We run to the open window to see a police car pulling up to the side of the road. It plays its siren again.

'I don't believe it—the powder didn't work!' I cry. 'Maybe I didn't give the Melkshams enough. They've sent the police. I have to warn Dad.'

'No!' Ethan races back to his bed and grabs hold of the mask. 'You have to help me hide your stuff. Grab your rucksack. It's in the corner. I'll get the laptop.'

'But the police won't come in here. They'll be safe. It's Dad that isn't.'

I climb onto the windowsill, about to jump onto the tree, when Ethan says, 'Scarlet.'

Something in his tone makes me turn around.

'The policeman isn't here for you,' he says. 'He's here for me.'

'What? He knows about your hacking?' I exclaim,

watching in horror as the car door opens. 'We have to get rid of your computer. We can take it back to mine. Help me carry it down the tree and you can hide there too.'

Ethan shakes his head. He looks like he's going to throw up. 'Please don't hate me.'

'Why would I hate you?'

'Because that policeman is my dad.'

It's as if time stands still. His words bounce off the four walls. I glance down at the tall muscular fair-haired man climbing out of the car and strutting to the door.

'That's your dad?' I whisper.

Ethan nods.

'Your dad is a *policeman*?' I feel my blood heating up, my wrist tightening.

Ethan nods again.

'How could you not tell me that?' My hands fly to my face. 'Is that why you helped me? To set me up? You wanted to get on the good side of your dad? Catch a cat burglar?'

'No!' says Ethan, looking horrified. 'I helped you to get back at him. I hate him. That's why I hack into computers too.'

'What?' I yell. The skin on my hands bubble and I don't trust myself. If I transform, I'm not sure what I'll do. I leap down from the windowsill and stand in front of Ethan's mirror. I stare at the reflection. My mouth is set in a grim line and my eyes are angry, hurt. Slowly my skin returns to normal but Ethan's words ricochet around my head. 'You helped me just to get back at him?'

Ethan nods, as the doorbell rings. I storm back over to the window and climb onto the ledge.

'Scarlet, please. Don't go. Just listen for a minute!'

I turn to face him.

Ethan takes a deep breath. 'That's why I helped you in the first place. Well . . . not the very first place. At the beginning I couldn't work out why you didn't want to be my friend. Most girls do. You intrigued me. I'd never met anyone like you—the way you acted.' He smiles pleadingly, as if hoping I might smile back. I glare at him and his face falls.

The doorbell rings again. Obviously Ethan's gran can't hear it.

Ethan continues: 'Then when I found out what you were, I thought—this is my chance. It was the perfect revenge against my dad, the policeman. I was going to help two cat burglars. But then I started liking you, really liking you. You became my friend. You are my friend.'

I snort. 'I thought you were my friend too. And after all that we just said—I was beginning to trust you.'

'You can trust me.'

'Do you know—you are the first person I was honest with since Mum died? You are the first person I let see the real me.' Tears prickle my eyes, and I wipe them away angrily. 'And all this time you were lying!'

'I wasn't!'

I hear the door open.

'Dad must have a key,' yelps Ethan, shoving my rucksack under his bed.

'I thought he was on a cruise. Or was that a lie too?' I demand.

'They must have come back early.' He stumbles over to the windowsill, his face white as a sheet. 'Scarlet, I really am sorry I never told you. I was planning to. When you and your dad were safe.'

I fight back the tears. 'Are you going to tell your dad about me? What I do?'

'No! Never!' says Ethan.

Then his eyes grow wet and he turns away. I can't help thinking how much he's helped me over the last few days. Maybe his motivations weren't pure, but then again, I was using him at the start too.

I soften my glare just as voices drift up the stairs.

'I'd better get going before your dad comes,' I croak.

'Well at least let me hide your stuff. I'll make sure Dad doesn't find it, I promise.'

'Yeah, OK,' I say. After all, I don't have time to shift it. 'I'll come back for it later, when it's safe.'

A tiny flicker of colour returns to his cheeks and he gives me a small smile. 'I'll leave the window open for you and I'll get Dad out of the house. I'll—I'll ask him if he wants to play football with me at the park.'

Whoa!

Ethan's words stop me in my tracks. Is he really offering to play football . . . *for me*? I don't think even Charlie or Jules ever did anything they didn't want to . . . *for me*.

I nod to him as a thank you, and leap onto the tree outside.

'See you later, Scarlet,' he says, his voice raw.

As I balance on the branch staring at him, I think about everything he's still willing to do for me.

'Actually Ethan,' I say, 'from now on, will you call me Scar?'

I flash him a smile and his face breaks into a sudden grin.

Then I slalom down the tree and I'm gone.

ABOUT THE AUTHOR

Having lived in several exotic places, Tamsin loves to travel, have adventures and see wild animals. She's swum with dolphins, ridden an elephant and held a seven-foot python. She lives in Somerset with her adrenalin-junkie family. When she isn't writing, she can be found tromping through the woods with her soppy dog, reading books or eating jellybeans.

AN INTERVIEW WITH
TAMSIN COOKE

Have you always wanted to be a writer?

I've made up stories since I was a little girl, but I didn't think about trying to become a writer until I was much older. It was only when I started scribbling down ideas and playing with stories, that I thought—this is something I would love to do!

Where did the idea come from for this book?

It all started with a dream. One night, I dreamt a bracelet sank into my bloodstream. I woke up feeling a bit shaken, but it got me thinking . . . Later that day, we went to Longleat Safari Park for my birthday. I saw so many different wild animals, and my mind started making leaps. Before I knew it, the seed was sown and Scar McCall was born.

What have you enjoyed most about working on this book?

Ooh—I've enjoyed so many things. I really liked researching the Aztecs, and learning about infamous heists. I loved discovering more about eagles and jaguars—how they move; how their senses work. But I think the thing I've enjoyed the most is getting to know my characters, Scar and Ethan. I loved seeing the exciting journeys they took me on. Often they surprised me.

What is the most interesting fact that you discovered when researching for the book?

Even though the Aztecs were a great fighting civilization, they adored beauty and nature. I find it fascinating that they believed warriors who died in battle would come back to life as hummingbirds or butterflies. I thought they would have chosen jaguars or eagles.

If you could shapeshift into any animal what would it be?

This is a really hard question because there are so many animals I would love to be. I would love to transform into an eagle so I could fly, or a dolphin so I could swim. But if I had to choose, I think I would be a lioness. Not only are they powerful, they have amazing night-vision, and the loudest roar of the cat family. They are incredibly sociable—hunting together, raising their young together. They also like lazing around, and sleeping lots!

We know that you love wild animals, but are there any animals that you're scared of?

Even though I've held snakes, stroked tarantulas, fed tigers, I'm too scared to touch a worm. I do like them. I just can't touch them. They're too wriggly and slimy!

ARE YOU READY FOR THE NEXT HEIST?

Dealing with the aftermath of wiped memories,
Scar struggles to keep her secrets safe.

Being demoted to mere lookout by her dad is a tough
pill to swallow but it's not long before she's swooping
and soaring into action once again.

But how will Scar cope when forced to make some
tough decisions, when she's not sure who she can trust?

Join Scar McCall on her next heist, out July 2016.

ACKNOWLEDGEMENTS

So many wonderful people have helped me bring this book to life.

My agent, Anne Clark, who was brave enough to take the plunge and who has held my hand throughout the whole process.

My editors Clare Whitston and Gillian Sore, who have endured endless emails, and helped shape and polish the text.

My husband, Graham, and my children, Toby and Daisy, who have listened to endless versions and spent many dinner times discussing possible twists and turns.

My sister, Pia Jones, who has been utterly truthful about my writing—sometimes to my horror!

My dad, Keith Jones, for being so enthusiastic.

Simon Harris, my neighbour, who has given me great insight into the mind of a cat burglar—if he wasn't a retired policeman, he would have made a very successful art thief!

Dr John Sullivan from Yale University for his Nahuatl translations. Any inaccuracies in the text are due to my over active imagination rather than the information from Dr Sullivan.

And finally **all my friends and family** who have been incredibly supportive from the very start. You know who you are!

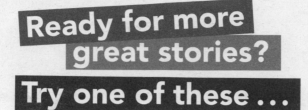